Spokes

Spokes

Stories from the Romani World

Janna Eliot

Five Leaves Publications
www.fiveleaves.co.uk

Spokes:
Stories from the Romani World
Janna Eliot

Published in 2008 by Five Leaves Publications,
PO Box 8786, Nottingham NG1 9AW
www.fiveleaves.co.uk

ISBN: 978 1 9055124 78

Five Leaves acknowledges financial support from
Arts Council England

Five Leaves is a member of Inpress (www.inpressbooks.co.uk),
representing independent publishers

Cover design: Darius Hinks
Typesetting: Four Sheets Design and Print
Printed in Great Britain

Thanks to Sara and Derek for their editing suggestions
and boundless support, and to everyone who inspired,
helped and encouraged me.

Contents

The Waiting

He waited.

His whole being concentrated on waiting.

He sent his spirit out to search the tracks, to listen for the sound of children's voices.

He waited. He waited for the running footsteps. He waited for the ringing laughter.

For the sun to shine again. For the moon to silver the night.

He watched the road in the winter, and in the summer.

He sat on the steps of his caravan, staring into the distance. The wooden plank dug into his bones, splintered his dreams. He waited for their return, the ones who'd been taken away.

He saw them, his Tutela, her bright skirts flapping in the wind, Kali, his wilful daughter, his beloved sons, and the little ones, Messelo and Sonia.

But the figures he saw advancing, running, dancing, laughing towards him always, always turned into evening shadows.

Sometimes he cradled his violin in his arms, stroking the strings, urging out soft vibrations to call them home. Sometimes he carved toys for them.

"Messelo loves dogs," he muttered, "let's make him a puppy. And this will be a lark for the baby."

He remembered Doosje's plump arms waving in her cradle.

The other Sinti Gypsies in the small encampment brought him food, cups of tea, twigs for the fire. They sat apart from him, talking softly to each other while he ate. Then, patting him on the back, or shaking his hand, they left him in peace.

He knew the lost ones would return.

It seemed so long ago, that day he'd been rehearsing for a wedding, practising a new tune with young Willy and Elmo, working on the rhythmic bass line. Usually alert to official visitors, they were so engrossed in the music that none of them heard the cars pull up.

And then Dutch police were across the encampment, picking up any man they could find.

His sons had managed to hide, but Moeselman and two of his brothers were handcuffed and marched away.

"We're sending you to a nice little place in the country for a rest!" sneered the policemen. "A lovely holiday home for Gypsies!"

The police station was full of angry Sintis. Cousins and uncles from other encampments. Friends last seen at a funeral.

He was a prisoner. Shaved, checked over and registered. Put on a train to Amersfoort. No way of escape. Days and nights spent praying his wife and children were safe.

He was sent to work in the great Philips' factory complex in Eindhoven. Moeselman was used to hard work, but not to this mindless discipline, the stupid rules, the numbers, the brutality. Like the rest of his group, he did the minimum possible, mechanically assembling components for aviation radio systems. Like the other prisoners, he sabotaged as many units as he could.

He watched for ways to escape, and when he saw there were none, he waited. He waited for the war to end.

At night in the barrack, he dreamwalked to his

family. He sent his spirit to find them. He sat round their fire, played them sweet music, held their hands. Tickled Doosje's plump cheeks.

He waited till they'd be together again.

The days were like long grey roads in winter, icy and rough. A gnawing hunger. A nagging ache. And then it was over. Moeselman stumbled out into the street with the comrades who'd survived beatings and starvation.

Somehow, he trudged back to Maastricht. Somehow, he acquired a caravan. Somehow, he knew his family would find him.

He waited. Watched and waited. He sat on the caravan steps in summer, squinting at the sunlit paths. He huddled by the stove in winter, gazing into the flames. What he saw in the fire was too dreadful to believe, too stark to contemplate.

The weeks went by. Others slipped back from the shadow world, quietly, with dead eyes, with blue marks on their skin. They whispered of tortures and torments, of hangings and shootings. They told of burnings and gassings, of rapes, of a child, a boy of two or three, tossed into an oven.

They mumbled as they talked and stumbled when they walked.

"They must be mad!" said those who had remained behind. "What they say can't be true!"

Barend told him there was a place, an office, which helped find missing relatives.

"Red Cross, they call it. I'll drive you."

Moeselman sat in the old car, staring out at the bombed streets, at the children eating weeds from wasteland, at thin women scrabbling in rubble for hidden treasure.

He hung back at the door. Offices meant trouble,

police checks, questions, shouts and prison, but this place was different. It was filled with tearful visitors and clerks who smiled.

The woman was kind. She gave him a pen and a form to fill in and showed him to a table.

Moeselman stared at the form. He could hear his father's voice inside his head. "I don't hold with reading, turns folk into zombies, zombies who can't think for themselves and who obey stupid laws. Us Sintis, we don't need to read. We remember everything. Names and tunes, places and numbers. Only idiots need to read."

Moeselman nodded. His father had been right. Nazis could read. They wrote everything down. They made lists.

"I can't read," he told Barend.

"I know, brother," Barend cleared his throat. "But I can read and write a bit. Tell me the names of your family."

Names. There were so many names. Secret names. False names. Official names. Sinti names, only used within the group.

"What are the names?" Moeselman mumbled. "I can't remember."

Names were shadows round camp fires, ghosts dancing at weddings, wraiths running beside a horse.

Dark sounds issued from the tomb of his mouth. "Kali, Willy, Doosje..."

He watched Barend's large hand trail blue scrawls across the page.

Haltingly, Barend read out the next question. "*Date of birth.* When were they born?"

Born? Moeselman closed his eyes, dreamwalking back to the past. It had been that time they called *before*, before the laws forbidding travel, before the registrations, before the German Occupation.

"Remember!" he whispered to himself. "You must remember."

He forced himself to float from the warm office. He felt cold flakes on his skin. He shivered. He could see snow.

It had been a cold winter, the coldest for fifty years, so they'd said in Grevenbicht. He could see the Christmas decorations in the church. There was Tutela in her long blue skirt and red scarf. And the godmother, the doctor's wife, holding the tiny infant.

What was that child called? Blieta, Settela, Marietta? What did it matter? You give a baby a name and it dies anyway, sooner or later.

He waited. He waited while Barend scribbled painstakingly on the white form, and handed it back to the clerk.

"We'll be in touch," the clerk promised, smiling. "As soon as we know anything, we'll let you know."

A pub. Cold eyes watching them. False smiles. Barend slapping coins on the counter. An old man coming over to shake hands and offer a drink. Waiting for the *genever*, feeling it burn his throat.

Back in the car, along dusty potholed roads, to the camp. Back to the caravan. To wait.

One day, a woman came with a photograph. A distant cousin, someone who'd hidden out during the Occupation.

A family photograph taken before the war. There he was, solid and square, with gleaming black hair and a neat moustache, as he stared out at the photographer. And there was Tutela, her scarf covering her chestnut hair, laughing. The children, nine of them, ranged in front. One of the boys, Messi perhaps, was twisting round, his face full of mischief.

Maybe they won't recognise me, he thought. When they come back. My hair is white. I'm an old man. My bones stick out of my hands.

Slowly, over the months, the Red Cross gave him answers he didn't want to hear. Answers full of madness. Answers howling an insane savage tale.

Answers that told him his wife had been gassed. That his sons were dead. That the girls were dead. That little plump Doosje had been murdered. Good children, all of them. The boys, Willy and Elmo, were those their names? Brilliant violinists, both of them. Dead.

The violin lay in his arms, silent. He ran his hand over its fragile neck. He tapped the beautiful brown body, the bridge, the strings, the lovely curve of the sound holes.

And he picked up his bow. There, sitting on the steps, he started to play. The first time he'd played since he'd come back.

The wind stopped whistling and the children from the encampment crept nearer. The women stopped shouting and sank onto their haunches, leaving clothes in the washtubs and pots boiling on the fires. The birds stopped singing in their cages. The men put down their tools and listened.

They waited. They waited until Moeselman had poured out his song and his life and his music and his anguish and his family and the trains and the fires and the gassing and the barbed wire and the tattoos and the madness and the savagery.

And when the tune was over, he laid his violin upon the grass, rested his bow across the instrument, and slowly, peacefully, looked up at the sky.

He stretched out upon the field, and died.

"He died of grief," they said later, "but there was a smile on his face."

There was a smile on his face. The waiting was over.

First Day at School

Maria was going to school. For the first time. She was scared.

The other children in the street weren't scared.

Maria thought this might be because their parents hadn't come from Poland after the war. But she wasn't sure.

Maria's mother was always scared. Papa said that was because in the war, she'd hidden in a barn in Central Europe.

That was because Mama was something called an undesirable. So she hid in a barn, and a kind Bavarian farmer and his wife looked after her and brought her food. Maria wasn't sure what an undesirable was, but it sounded horrible. She didn't know what a Bavarian farmer was either, but that sounded nice.

"Mama crouched behind hay bales, night after night, listening to the bombs falling," Papa explained. "When the farmer's wife brought her a lantern, shadows flickered on the barn walls. Mama was so scared she longed to die. That's why she shouts at us sometimes."

Maria's hair was very long and thick. She wore it in plaits which Mama threaded with ribbons. "The old Gypsy style," Mama called it. Maria loved her pretty ribbons. None of the other girls in the street had ribbons like her. Sunita had black plaits too, but they were fastened with plain elastic bands or dull brown wool. Only Maria had beautiful ribbons.

Every night, something scary happened. It wasn't as scary as hiding in a barn, but Maria didn't like it. It was when Mama sat her in front of the kitchen fire and loosened her braids. Then she tugged the comb through Maria's hair. It really hurt.

As Mama combed, she told stories in a mixture of Polish, Romani and English about drowned children and kidnapped maidens and handsome heroes. Maria was scared of the witches and the magic houses that could walk. She wept silently as Mama recited poems of speaking birds and wood goblins that lured little children to their death.

At the end of the combing, the torn-out hair was thrown into the fire. Sizzling, it flew up the chimney, leaving an acrid, sweet smell. The smell made Maria feel sick.

Huge shadows flickered on the wall, giving the night a sense of drama and dark legend. Sometimes, when she heard footsteps running past the front door, Maria tensed, waiting for soldiers to burst in and drag her away.

Mama couldn't read English very well. She sat at the table, whispering words from the newspaper to herself. That was normal. Most of the children in Maria's street had parents like that, parents who couldn't read English properly.

When Mama got angry, Maria wanted to escape and hide in a barn, only there weren't any barns in London. Then the kitchen walls closed in on her, like a prison cell. The angry shouts and silences stifled her. Sometimes she didn't dare breathe in case her breathing dislodged the flimsy structure of her life, making it crash down.

Janusz said school was all right. You just had to be careful not to upset the teachers. You got homework about Tudor Britain. Sometimes Maria helped him colour in pictures of timbered houses and women in lovely dresses.

Janusz wasn't afraid of Mama. He said she was funny. He mocked her, copying her foreign accent and throwing up his arms. That made Maria laugh.

It was her first day at school. Maria was scared.

"Come, I make hair," Mama said. She tugged Maria's hair, straining it at the roots. Each time the comb struck a tangle in the sleep-ruffled locks, Mama shouted a command.

"Don't be naughty!" The comb swept downwards.

"Don't be late!" Down went the comb again.

"Don't answer the teacher back!"

Maria's plaits were braided so tightly, she couldn't move her eyebrows.

"It hurts, Mama," she whimpered.

But Mama kept on plaiting. "Behave yourself on the school!" she said. "You doing bad thing, peoples say you dirty Polska Gypsy!"

Papa gave Maria a shiny new coin to spend on the way home. "This is a special day, Maria darling. Your first day. You're a big girl now!"

Janusz was right. School was nice. Maria's teacher, Miss Parry, was smiley and kind, and Sunita and Kevin from the street were in her class. They listened to stories and drew pictures. In Music, Maria was handed a drum. She banged it loudly as they all marched around the hall.

At break, she ran into the playground with her friends, shouting and laughing. "Come and skip!" called Sunita, getting out a rope.

Maria and Fatima jumped together as the others sung the skipping tune.

> *My mother said*
> *I never should*
> *play with the Gypsies in the wood.*
>
> *If I did*
> *she would say*
> *naughty little girl to disobey.*

In the afternoon, they had Quiet Time. "Choose a book from the shelves and look at the pictures," Miss Parry said. Maria was very tired and sleepy. Taking the coin from her pocket, she thought about the Lucky Dip bag of sweets she was going to buy after school. Her mouth watered.

Something clanged. The coin had slipped out of her fingers and rolled across the carpet. It glinted dully in the afternoon sun, like an accusing eye.

"Oh! Someone's dropped some money!" exclaimed Miss Parry. "Whose is it?"

Nobody moved. Maria's heart beat quicker, shaking her body. She couldn't breathe. She didn't dare speak in case the teacher said she was trying to steal the money, like a dirty Polska Gypsy.

A thin boy with grimy marks round his neck put up his hand.

"Please, Miss," he whined. "It's mine!"

As Maria watched Miss Parry hand him the money, a horrible taste burnt her throat. The taste of disappointment. The taste of injustice. The taste of fear.

Midnight Mother

Per is looking out of the window, at the snowy garden and the starry sky.

From Mor's bedroom comes a rhythmic snore. The sound is like the noise of bellows. The image of a man fanning the flames of a fire springs into his head.

He smiles at his reflection in the darkened window, running his fingers through his red hair. When he winks, a deep blue eye winks back at him.

"You're a has been," he tells himself. "Life has passed you by. You're getting old! Going bald!"

"We chose you because of your thick curly hair," Mor had always told him. "You were the most handsome lad in the Oslo Home, and you smiled so sweetly. You held your arms up to us. Erik and me, we knew you were the one for us."

He smiles again, remembering Mor before she became old and ill. How she used to collect him after school, straight from work, full of gossip and smelling of fish. And the good times he spent with Far on the farms in the holidays, picking fruit or delivering milk churns.

His hair started thinning after Far died, when everything started going wrong. When Mor had a stroke, and Magda left for America.

A dog barks further down the lane. Torkel's labrador, always wakeful and on guard. Probably seen a fox.

Per flexes his shoulders, looks down at his hands. Although he'd given them a good scrubbing after work, car-grease lines his fingernails. Quietly, he goes to the bathroom and fills the sink with water.

He splashes his face, examining it carefully. He notes the wrinkles on his forehead, the lines running from nose to chin. He smooths his greying moustache. Outlandish face, he thinks.

He looks a bit like his father, his stepfather that is. Nearly ten years now since Far died. Nearly ten years since Mor had a stroke. Nearly ten years since Magda went away.

An old towel hangs on the bathroom door. He scrapes it over his face, rubbing vigorously. Enough of this self pity, he tells the image in the mirror. You have friends in the village, you coach the football team, you like your job in the garage. You have fun playing with the band.

As he walks past the half-open door, Mor calls out in her sleep. Per creeps to her bedside, straightens the blanket. A patch of moonlight is shining on the bed.

"What will I do when you're gone, Mor?" he thinks. "You've always loved and cherished me. I know adopted children are meant to feel a lack, a hole in their lives, a desperation, but I've always been content. Even when I wasn't too good at school, you just said, 'Well, no one in our family's ever been cut out for book learning. We'll get you an apprenticeship, you can work on a farm like your Dad.'"

He walks silently back to the front room, his slippered feet brushing across the wooden floor.

In the end he'd got a job at the local garage, with Swedish Bengt. Bengt was a great boss, took Per under his wing and taught him all he knew. Bengt had no living relatives, so when he retired, he gave the business to Per.

"Well done, son," Far had said. "I'm proud of you."

Mor had made a cloudberry torte to celebrate, and invited Bengt to dinner. Magda had come too, her hair gleaming in the candlelight.

Far had opened a bottle of aquavit. "A toast to Bengt for a happy retirement, and to my son for his success."

"And good luck to the happy couple," Mor added. "You'll be able to tie the knot soon, now that Per's doing so well."

Magda couldn't wait to leave Norway and go to America. Even at primary school, when she was asked what she was going to be, she always answered, "An American."

She worked her way up in one of the big Norwegian banks in town, applying for a training scheme in America. Just before Far's death, she was transferred to the bank's Manhattan branch. Per agreed it made sense for her to go and start earning big bucks, find a flat, get settled. He'd follow when he'd sold the business.

"I'll come back twice a year," he promised his parents. "And I'll send tickets for you to visit us at Christmas and Midsummer. You won't notice I've gone!"

But he never got to America. First Far died, then Mor became ill. He couldn't leave his mother, there was no question about it.

"There's a really good Old Peoples' Home in Prestfoss, just an hour or so from Oslo," Magda had written from Manhattan, but Per wouldn't abandon

Mor. He owed her too much. And there was another thing. He couldn't imagine living in the States. He'd never really got on with the English language, and his friends said he'd find life in America too hectic and work centred.

He settles in the chair and sighs. "I'm happy enough here," he murmurs. "I've got my mother, my guitar, my work."

This is something he recites several times a week. Usually he believes what he's saying, but tonight, his words sound false.

He turns to look at the guitar hanging on the hook on the wall. Ragnhild and Olaf are getting married next week, and the band's been booked to play.

He damps down the longing in his stomach. When Magda wrote to say she was marrying a Norwegian-American, he wasn't really surprised. And he didn't really care. Magda had become a habit, an assumption.

"My son, my dear boy, I've ruined your life," Mor wept when he read her the blue airmail letter.

"Nonsense, Mor. If you hadn't taken me in, who knows what would have happened, where I'd have ended up! You hear stories about adopted kids being treated as slaves, made to work all day on allotments, left to sleep in outhouses. You cosseted me. I could never leave you."

The moon gleams brighter, and the dog down the lane barks louder. Per glances out of the window again, wondering what the labrador has seen.

If things had been different, he thinks, I might have been a pop star by now.

He stands up to get the guitar, and strums gently, humming one of the old tunes he'd made up so long ago. A song for Magda. He'd written it one

Midsummer, when the sun hung in the sky all day and all evening too, when the air was full of music and love. *Midsummer Magda*, he'd called it.

He stops playing. There's a movement in the garden.

He checks his watch. Midnight. The line between night and day. The magic time, Mor calls it.

He waits for the spell to break.

There are figures walking up the path, leaving footprints in the snow. He hurries into the hall, picking up a walking stick.

He throws the door open. Before him stands an elderly woman, wearing a long skirt and a wide-sleeved jacket. A scarf covers her head. Her eyes are dark, glowing in the starlight. A foreigner.

Time stands still. Per puts down the stick. The wind blows into the warm house.

He knows what she's going to say. Her voice fills his dreams. A soft, melodious voice, one that has always crooned silently inside his head.

"My son, I've been looking for you for forty-five years. They took you from me. I had no choice."

A man comes forward and clasps his hand. "I'm Mikael, your brother."

The younger woman is small. Her eyes are deep blue. "I'm Gunnil, your sister."

They all stare at each other, he inside the house, bathed in the light of the hall, they waiting in the snow, gilded by moonbeams.

"Come in," he says. "My mother's asleep, she's ill, we mustn't wake her."

The visitors take off their wet boots, their shawls and hats, and follow him silently into the kitchen. Per gets cups, fills the jug, spoons coffee, trying to make sense of the questions standing behind him.

There's a weight in his stomach.

"I knew I was adopted," he says, "but I was told my parents were dead."

He cannot believe the betrayal. That he had, has always had a family. Another family. One he never even realised he yearned for.

How could Far and Mor have done this to me?

His hand shakes as he swirls the liquid in the jug.

"We were not dead!" says the older woman. Her voice breaks. "Your father was Norwegian, a sailor. I was selling flowers in the market. We fell in love. One night, he was arrested, imprisoned for drunkenness and assault. I was pregnant. When you were born, the nurse took you away. In those days, in the sixties and seventies, the Norwegian authorities took away mixed race Gypsy children. But I never stopped looking for you."

She holds his hand.

"You are a Gypsy?" he queries. "I am a half-Gypsy?"

Somehow he has always known this. He's heard it in the birdsong and in the warm breeze and in the chords of the guitar. In the sagas they recited at school. In the laughter that sometimes roars through him. In horizons and wide open spaces.

"You are my mother? You're my brother and sister? I thought I had no blood relatives..."

He's surrounded, hugged, embraced. They wipe away his tears. His mother puts her hands to his cheeks.

"Forty-five years I have searched for you, and at last I've found you."

She whispers something that he doesn't understand. Another language. He grasps her hand. Her fingers, like his, are long and calloused with work.

He tries not to cry. "Where have you been, all these years? They said you were dead."

The woman's eyes are as bleak as a winter night.

"I was so ill when they took you away. They kept me in hospital for weeks, and later, when I was well enough to ask, they said you'd been given to a family in Sweden. I went to Sweden, to my sister's house, and got married. I had four more babies, two died, but Gunnil and Mikael survived. And I always kept looking for you."

Gunnil, his sister, speaks. Her Norwegian is tinged with a strange accent.

"It was me who said we should try to find you, to look for you in Norway where you were born," she says. "It's different now, people are more open, we young ones can read and write, the authorities can't brush us away like they did our parents."

The older woman rubs her hand along his jaw.

"What are your foster parents like? Do they love you? Do they treat you well?"

Per's voice rises from some deep fiord.

"My father..." He glances at the woman. "My step-father died some years ago, a heart attack. My ... Mor is very ill, she has high blood pressure, she needs a lot of care."

Anguished, he adds, "I can't leave her."

I want to come with you, he thinks. I belong with you.

"Son, we haven't come to steal you away. We've only come to tell you we are your family. Your other family. I had to find you, to let you know I never stopped thinking of you. Your Mor needs you, but maybe sometimes we can meet?"

They finish their drinks, put on their outdoor clothes.

"What did they name you?" asks the woman as he opens the door. It is snowing again, and a few flakes whirl in from the garden.

"Per," he replies.

"I called you Elias," she whispers.

They disappear into the night. Where are you staying, he wants to shout after them, when will I see you again?

In the morning, Per gives Mor her medication. He tells her about the night-time visitors. She is shocked and ashamed. The tablet falls onto the coverlet. She stares at him in horror.

"No! It can't be true! They told me your parents were dead! How could I have stolen a child from its mother? I know the pain of being childless. I could never have done that to another woman. There were papers, it was legal. Before she died, your mother signed papers..."

He knows she is retelling what she had been told. He puts his arms around her thin shoulders. "Mor, they're coming back. They want to meet you. They want our two families to be friends."

A card comes later, suggesting a day for a visit.

Mor becomes stronger. She struggles to get dressed, sends Per out for flour, cream, eggs and a packet of frozen mixed berries. He watches her beat and stir the mixture and smooth it into a tin. The kitchen fills with the warm scent of childhood as the cake swells and firms.

Mor taps the cake from the tin, inverting it onto the wire cooling-rack. Later she spreads cream on top, swirls red strawberries and golden cloudberries over the surface.

He has seen her do this many times, but today is different. He coughs and clears his throat.

His mother hobbles to answer the door. Her shiny black dress hangs like a tent round her thin frame. He sees the other mother reach out to clasp her. Gunnil is standing behind her.

Mor weeps. "I didn't know, please believe me, I would never have stolen a child. Although I was so empty and sad, I couldn't have lived with myself…"

"It is not your fault," the visitor says as Mor leads her into the kitchen. "They lied to us both. They lied to us all. But I love you for caring for my boy. He is a beautiful son, our beautiful son."

"They showed me your signature, your agreement."

"But I cannot read or write! I never signed anything. I would never have given away my son."

"What shall I call you?" Per asks. He feels burdened. Two mothers. One Norwegian, one Gypsy.

"The others call me Dei," the woman replies. "It's the word for Mor in our language."

"Dei." He tries the word in his mouth. It feels like a frozen berry, hard and cold. "Dei."

Gunnil smiles at Per. "Mikael had to go to Oslo today. But he wants to meet you next Saturday. There's a gathering in Strømstadt. That's a camp where the stolen children meet up.There are thousands of them, discovering their true background at last. A man called Olof, one of the stolen ones, started this place, a centre to meet at weekends, to learn about Traveller and Gypsy culture. Mikael and me go there to help. I give Romani language and dance lessons, my brother teaches traditional crafts."

Per pours coffee, Mor cuts the cake. Her hand trembles and the knife clatters back onto the tray. It's a wooden tray Per made at school, with carved leaves and berries around the rim. In a graceful, easy gesture, Gunnil gets to her feet and finishes dividing the cake, slipping the slices onto plates.

"Delicious!" the visitors comment. "You are a wonderful cook."

Mor smiles and offers them another slice.

A forest. A long track. Pine edged paths. Ramblers with instruments and backpacks.

Mikael is striding beside him. Per stops. He cannot make this journey. It's too far. It will take him to another place, another country. He is Norwegian. He has always been Norwegian. He doesn't need another path.

Gunnil is talking to a middle-aged woman. A plump, plain woman with kind brown eyes.

Gunnil beckons him over. "This is Karolin," she says. "It's her first time too."

Karolin grasps his hand firmly and shakes it up and down. "I'm really nervous," she confides. Her voice is low and breathy. "I only found out about my past a few months ago. It's all so new and strange. One day I'm the manager of a supermarket, a woman in a suit with a mortgage, and the next day I discover I'm the daughter of a Traveller, a *Reisende* who ran a fairground in Denmark. Unbelievable."

Per nods. He understands how she feels. Behind torn curtains lurk long hidden treasures and truths. Myths. Traditions. Lies.

They follow the others to a clearing where a tall man is waiting. "That's Olof, the guy who started this group," explains Mikael.

Olof begins to speak. "This is the site of an old Gypsy encampment. Ghosts of the past roam here. Ghosts of travelling people killed by the government's fear of nomadism."

Per looks around. Some of the listeners have their eyes closed, others stare into the distance. He bends his head and looks at the grass.

"Fear destroys. During those dreadful years, not so long ago, we lost our children, our horses, our language and our songs. Stolen by the State."

Per looks up. This is all new for him. He thought Gypsies were feckless people who roamed the countryside in caravans and sang happy songs. That's what Mor and Far had always told him. That's what he'd learnt at school, seen in films. He knew nothing about this history of violence and State theft.

"We are the stolen children." Olof's voice rises. "Ripped from our parents because one of them was a Gypsy or Traveller. Many of us are confused. We don't know who we are. We've only just learnt of our true ancestry, we feel bereft. That's why I started this club..."

Per looks at the pine trees, the blue sky between the black-green branches. Larks and swallows swoop, circle, call and wheel away. He realises he's clinging to Karolin's hand, like a drowning man to a rope.

"We, the stolen children, have come to reclaim our heritage. To learn our songs, our dances, our lost language."

Smoke rises from the candles to the resin scented pines. Per looks at his companions and sees in their eyes something he hasn't felt for years. Hope.

Music wafts into his head. A new tune. A song about a long winding road. About a plain dark-haired wife with kind eyes. About a plump baby, and summers trekking around the lakes and forests of his beautiful country.

He'll call the song *Midnight Mother*.

Fire in the Belly

No one would have called Martha Murphy beautiful, but nor was she ugly. Homely she was, with lank brown hair and eyes the colour of the Irish Sea.

She had arrived in London at the age of eighteen, fresh from the children's home in County Cork, to make her fortune.

She worked in shoe shops, baker shops, flower shops, newsagents, butchers' shops and as a cleaner in a hospital.

Finally, after marrying Patrick, a Wickford man employed in the building trade, she had two children and took a job in Tesco.

Although her body thickened after pregnancy and with the passage of time, Martha liked nothing better than a bit of a *houli*. She went to all the *ceilidhs* organised at the church, and most Saturday nights found her at the Molti Mar in Holloway where the Irish bands played.

Even when she was cooking, Martha Murphy danced. She stepdanced with her daughter Josi in the kitchen while the potatoes were boiling, drumming out familiar rhythms with her feet.

The son Mark took up an engineering apprenticeship and went to live in Glasgow, where he married a pretty lass whose people came from Connemara. Then Josi went to Bath University to study Media and IT, and it was quiet in the house without the hip-hop blaring away and the school friends flocking into the kitchen in search of a feed.

It was after they'd driven Josi up to Bath with all her luggage, and returned to the empty house, that Martha started to change.

"The children are doing so well," she remarked to Pat, filling the kettle."Sure it's lonely and quiet, but isn't that what we left Ireland for, to better ourselves? And the kids, it's grand they've the choice now, they can do what they want. Not like us."

A drop of water spilled onto her finger, and she turned off the tap, thinking of life on the side of the road. Before the nuns had taken her away. Before Mammy died.

It had been Martha's job go to the standpipe twice a day, to fill the water buckets. In wind, in snow, in summer heat.

"We wouldn't want that for our children," she said out loud.

Pat grunted and slurped his tea. Billy called to take him to the pub, leaving Martha alone. After Coronation Street, she switched off the box and prowled the house, first standing next to Mark's bed, then going into Josi's room, running her hands over the mirror.

"Sure, I'm dreadful lonely," she told her reflection, wondering what the children were doing. She rubbed her tears away with plump fingers and went down to the kitchen. There, she slotted a Matt Cunningham tape into the cassette player, and danced and danced, whirling round to lose herself in the beat.

"Something'll turn up," she chanted. "I can feel it in me bones."

Next day, on the bus to work, she saw a bright yellow leaflet lying on an empty seat.

**RAQS SHARQI
7.30pm EVERY TUESDAY.
BULL THEATRE ANNEXE.
MOVE YOUR BODY TO EASTERN RHYTHMS**. **BEGINNERS WELCOME**.

Martha picked up the leaflet and nodded to herself. It was a sign. She didn't go to theatres, but she knew The Bull. It was in the High Street, between Lloyds Bank and the Post Office.

I'll take a look next week, she thought.

The annexe, a prefabricated building at the back of The Bull car park, reminded her of the school for Traveller kids she'd attended back home. A ramshackle shed where a nice old lady had taught her reading and writing.

Smiling at the memory, she pushed open the door. Inside the large room, a dozen women of all ages and races were chatting and laughing. They wore exotic clothes, full-length silk dresses or floating harem trousers and beaded tops. Martha sidled in, awkward in her brown pleated skirt and lace up shoes.

She stood next to an elderly woman who was draping a golden scarf round her thick waist. The woman smiled. "Hi! I'm Mina. Is this your first time? Do you need a wrap? I always bring a spare."

She offered Martha a blue veil edged with tiny silver bells.

"Thanks," said Martha, fingering the delicate material. The cloth was like the offering Mammy used to drape on the sacred tree near St. Declan's Well each summer. Not that the pilgrimage had done much good, mind. Mammy had died of the cancer anyway, and all the kids had been taken into care.

Martha shuddered.

Mina crinkled her eyes. "Don't worry, my dear, you'll be fine."

Martha nodded shyly, knotting the blue veil round her hips. "I'm not sure if I should be here. I'll probably be useless."

A striking blonde in a floor length black dress and scarlet sequinned shawl took her place at the front of the class.

"That's Marina, the teacher," Mina explained.

"We'll start as usual with stretching exercises," Marina said. "New people, take it easy, just copy what you can. Don't strain. It'll come in time."

The room was filled with the haunting sounds of Egyptian music. At first Martha stood still, lost in pleasure at the warm, complex sounds. Marina was moving her hip up and down, in a one two three rhythm — not unlike a jig. Martha copied, extending her arm like the teacher, stroking the air, framing her body, writhing like a snake as she turned round.

"Have you done this before?" Marina asked Martha in the short break.

"Never. I only do the Irish dancing."

"You're very good, you've got an obvious feel for it."

Martha smiled. The flowing movements suited her hips and wide-boned frame.

When they had to wobble their stomachs, Martha got another compliment from Marina and felt ridiculously proud. She made her tummy shake like jelly, her arms soft and floaty like branches in a gentle breeze.

Wafting home like an Eastern princess, drumbeats

in her ears, she found Pat brewing up some tea.

"Where've you bin, darlin'? I was worrying about you."

"I was at a dance class, didn't I tell ye?"

"Sure you did. Now, will I do you a bit of bread and sugar?"

Next day at the Tesco check out, Martha found herself humming snatches of Egyptian tunes. As she waited for customers, she flexed her body, her fingers drumming Arabic riffs on the rubber conveyor. At lunchtime, she hurried to the local market and bought lengths of bright green chiffon and satin.

The week floated by. In her spare time, when Pat was at work, she practised moves. She bought a tape of Turkish music from the Albanian shop down the road and made up new steps, combining Eastern movements with intricate Irish jigs.

When it was time for the next class, she felt she was stepping back into reality. Classmates looked up as she went into the Annexe, smiling as if she was part of their sisterhood. Wasn't it great to have a place where men couldn't enter, where she could move her body, enjoying her power, where it wasn't a sin to shake her chest.

She knotted her emerald scarf around her waist, waiting for the class to start. Stretching her arms, she moved her lower body in a figure of eight, isolating her hips in the one two three beat.

"We're doing camels today," Marina said, demonstrating the movement. "Push your stomach out, crunch down, then pull it in, hollowing your back at the same time. Repeat."

The folds of Martha's skin concertinaed as she compressed her stomach, throwing her spine free and straight as she stretched. She could do camels

forever, she felt, riding the movement through the
desert of life everlasting. She smiled as she repeated
the steps, rippling her trunk in the treacly sinuous
movement.

Autumn was fading into winter. Josi would be home
soon, and Mark would bring Bridget down from
Scotland for Christmas.

Martha stood in front of the bedroom mirror,
shaking her shoulders, circling them in turn, fluttering them quicker and quicker, wiggling her
collarbone so it took on a life of its own.

Won't Josi be impressed, she thought, as she prac-
ticed the Kenya. She could hear Marina's instructions.
"Hip swivel to the left, crunch, to the right, crunch,
move your foot in opposition to your shoulders."

Martha looked in the mirror, feeling that the staid
matron was turning back into a bright-eyed girl.

She had her nose pierced one Saturday, when Pat
was working down in Dagenham. She started to wear
long golden earrings, enjoying the sensation of cool
metal against her neck. She thought she looked exciting, mysterious, although Pat said he preferred her
as she'd been before.

"Aren't I the same woman?" she laughed. "I just
want to be a bit more interesting."

"You've always looked grand to me," he commented, kissing her greying hair.

It was January, the first class of the Spring Term.
Martha walked through The Bull car park, squeezed
past an old wreck dumped by Christmas joyriders,
pushed open the door and greeted her friends.

Hypnotised by throbbing music, she echoed the
rhythm of the drum with her bare feet. They were
doing veil work this week, and Martha waved her sari

remnant behind her like the sail of a ship.

"Veils to the left, to the right, and over your head," called Marina.

The music grew louder and louder, filling the small prefab with magic.

Mina was the first to notice. "Smoke!" she shouted, but her voice was lost in the sobbing lute and cymbals. Martha was enthralled by the music, the waving scarves, the chiming bells. She vaguely saw Marina open the door and the whisk of an orange scarf as the teacher fled into the night.

Bright flames of gold and silver, crimson and purple licked the room. The remaining dancers wrapped their veils around their mouths and heads and dashed through the door, past the blazing wreck.

"Martha!" she heard Mina scream.

"Martha!" her classmates yelled.

And through the smoke and the fire, the throb of the drums and the lute, Martha caught the wail of a siren as she spun round and round like a burning candle.

The Sound Effect

Matthew wiped his face with a freshly laundered handkerchief.

It was hot in the studio, and the interview wasn't going as he wanted. He couldn't remember the last time he'd had such an annoying guest.

It had seemed such a good idea to invite a musician from the era of silent movies to talk about the past. "An authentic voice, a hidden layer of meaning!" That's what he'd said at the planning meeting.

Glancing at the old man sitting opposite, he started again.

"If you could just stick to the point, Boris!" he said politely. "Otherwise, we'll run out of time."

The old man laughed. "Time! You young people — always running after time. I'm sorry for you time chasers."

The guest was wearing shabby trousers, and a jacket obviously picked up from Oxfam. He had a ridiculous white beard, and long hair tied back in a ponytail. An earring in the left ear.

Matthew wiped his sweating hands on his well-pressed jeans, and nodded to the technician. "Roll!"

When he leaned forward, his sharp collar dug into his neck. "So how did you become a musician in the silent movies?"

"Now you're asking!" Boris replied. "Well, it was like this. Me mum made me go to school, but I left as soon as I could. Suppose you've been to University yourself, got a degree?"

Matthew nodded, masking his impatience. It wasn't done to let interviewees turn attention to the host. "And afterwards?" he prompted.

"Got a job as a trainee electrician!" declared Boris triumphantly.

A voice spoke through the earpiece clamped round Matthew's head. "Hurry him along."

Before Matthew could ask another question, Boris started talking again. "So, one day I bump into Fred. He's carrying an old flute case, humming a tune to himself."

Don't sing it, please don't sing it, Matthew begged silently.

Boris whistled a snatch of *Danny Boy*, warbling the last two bars.

"How yer doin', mush?" I ask him. 'I'm fine meself,' he says.

Then he says, 'Still got your old violin? They're looking for fiddlers down Cassells' Agency. Good dosh for geezers who know how to play!'"

At last, thought Matthew. He's finally going to tell me something interesting. The essentials of the situation.

"So that's how I come to hang up me overalls to play in the silent flicks. I knew how to play better than most, if I do say so meself!"

Boris leaned back in his chair, just out of camera focus, his eyes gleaming. Matthew gestured him to sit upright, and waited for the old man to continue.

"Me dad had come over from Russia, see. In the 1920s it must have been. One of a group of Gypsies — Roma you have to say nowadays. They were in a band. Played weddings and funerals for all the East

Europeans in London. He could fair make the fiddle sing, he could."

His faded brown eyes creased in concentration. "Hang on, I tell a lie, around 1914, it would have been, when he come over. Just before the Revolution. Anyway, to get back to the story."

Please do, thought Matthew.

"I goes down Cassells with Fred, gets taken on as a movie musician. Grand life, playing the pits. Thought I'd died and gone to heaven! No more working in empty, draughty houses. No more climbing up ladders or leaning into corners to drill holes for wiring."

Demonstrating the dangerous manoeuvre, Boris leaned to the left, almost falling off his chair. Matthew jumped up to support him.

"Nice one!" commented the voice in his earpiece. "We'll keep that in. Human interest."

Boris adjusted the belt of his trousers and resettled himself. "We sat in warm cinemas, on velvet seats — comfortable dark red seats. Not like these..." He pointed scornfully at the angular metallic studio chairs. "And I did what I really enjoyed. Playing the fiddle."

He picked up an imaginary violin and gave a few sweeps with an invisible bow. The action was so lifelike, Matthew could hear the sound of music in the studio.

"Can you explain how you were allocated to the various cinemas? I'm sure our viewers would love to know the details."

"It was like this, son. Every Monday morning, we'd go down Cassells in Archer Street. 'Spect you know where that is?"

Matthew shook his head.

"Well, it's just off Tottenham Court Road, between the Tube and Leicester Square. Anyway, the other musicians would be there. All me mates. Fred with his flute, Yosef with a big drum, Barney on double bass, and Femi, this big bloke from Nigeria, with a kora. They always asked for Femi for them African films."

Matthew wasn't sure what a kora was, but didn't interrupt. He nodded to his subject to continue. This was going well. If only he could avoid more demonstrations and diversions.

"So we all waits in the street, rain or shine. Then out comes old Mr. Gardner with a list, and yells out the names of the cinemas and the musicians they need for that day's films. Bit like a shopping list."

Boris laughed, a cackling old man's laugh, and Matthew grinned.

"Yeah, he'd call out like this." Boris put on a posh voice. "Wardour Street Odeon, two violins, one cello, one flute. Oxford Street Gaumont, one kora, pianist, double bass and sax."

He picked up the imaginary violin again.

"Good violinists were always in demand — you can do a lot with a fiddle, lad. Horror film — spooky effect made by running the wood of the bow across the strings. Tragedy, deep strokes for a weepy effect, staccato plucking for comedy."

Boris demonstrated, singing a few snatches to illustrate each point.

"So I was never out of work." He sighed, and fingered his beard. "Ah, it was a great life. Most of the lads' parents had come to London from far away. From places where the folk tradition was still strong. Didn't matter that Femi's old man was from a village near Lagos, or that my folks once travelled round

Russia in a caravan, or Fred's dad was from Donegal. We shared a common background, see — music."

This is great, Matthew thought. Ethnomusical background, just what we want. This programme's going to be hot.

The old man went on speaking, his face glowing. "I'll try to explain what it was like, setting up the music-stands in the pit. You got a real buzz, waiting for the red light to come on. You were in the middle, see, caught between the audience and the screen. We'd have a quick butchers at the script and play the appropriate tune. You've seen those old movies. Deanna Durban combing her hair, and then the villain steals up behind her. Cue for spooky music. Words flash up. I WILL NOT SUBMIT TO YOUR WICKED ADVANCES. Then we plays an exciting flourish."

His arm swept up and down, bowing the tune, his body stretching and turning with the melody.

"And when the heroine's tied to the railway lines, and the train comes bearing down, we're ready with that old favourite. *Diddle diddle dee, diddle diddle dee, bom bom bom bom bom bom bom bom.* Magic."

Matthew smiled with recognition, humming along quietly. He imagined himself in the darkened movie hall, playing the pit.

"Yeh," Boris went on. "And don't forget the classic death scene, when the beautiful girl's dying of consumption. That was my speciality, there was a weeping, *Da da, da — da da da da.*"

As if dancing, he wrung tears from the strings of his nonexistent violin.

"How can I explain it to you, a young fella brought up with all this modern technology? Now it's all buttons and electronics, no emotion! But back then...

We was touched with glamour. When I looked in the mirror, I saw a rough bloke with black hair, dark skin and slanting black eyes. I'd be the first too admit I'm no pin up. More like Charlie Chaplin."

He looked at Matthew for confirmation.

"Well, yes, I can see some similarity," Matthew agreed. "I can imagine, when you were younger..."

"The thing was, no matter what you looked like, you were sitting at the feet of the greats. There they were, day after day, film stars — faces made famous by the screen machine, their gestures, their actions, all larger than life. And I was part of their life."

This is it, Matthew thought. The essence of my programme. The influence of the screen machine on the common man.

"So," he commented, "this proximity to Hollywood gave your own life a drama and intensity that it wouldn't otherwise have had."

Boris blinked. "Sounds grand when you put it like that, lad, but yes, we did feel special, blessed. You never knew what was going to happen next, the movie might be set in America, Africa, France or Spain. You had to swap styles and music on demand. Once we played for *Slow Boat*, had to do Chinese music, like this."

He opened his mouth and mimicked a percussion instrument in a five-note scale.

"Pizzicato effect, they calls that. Better than wiring houses. That was all green, yellow, red wires, earthing cables. Boring. Down to earth, see."

He winked at Matthew. "Down to earth, get it?"

Matthew shrugged. "So what was it like being part of a tightly knit band of professionals?"

"Band of professionals, eh?" Boris repeated. "Sounds like the name of a film, don't it? We'd go down the pub, the *Black Horse* in Bow Street or *The Ship* in Islington, bit rough for the likes of you — anyway, they've all bin pulled down now for yuppie housing. We'd open the scores and discuss the routines. The dough was good too, better than the pay of a spark."

The producer's voice buzzed in the background and Matthew interrupted.

"I'll just explain to our younger viewers that a spark is an electrician."

Boris went on. "Every Wednesday, me old Dad rolled up to see the film. He'd come down the local with us after to give his tuppence worth. Always had something to say."

He switched into a heavy Russian accent.

"Zis when baby fall from pram, no enough filling. And when boy running from policemens, no good...."

Boris's face softened. "He'd take me fiddle, wave me bow around to explain a point. Then he'd forget what he was saying, and give us one of his old Gypsy tunes. The whole pub'd fall silent while me Dad was playing, and after, punters would cheer and get him a drink."

"Move him on, Matthew, don't let him repeat himself."

Matthew waved at the producer through the glass partition.

"So, Boris, tell me about your home life, your family."

"Loretta was the cashier at the Gaumont in Brewster Street," Boris answered. "A beauty, Italian parents, looked a bit like me Mum, she did. In them days you had to get wed before... well, you gets me drift. So we started courting, found a small house, slapped down a deposit on the rent and got hitched. I had everything I'd ever wanted, a great wife, a good job, and me own place."

Matthew relaxed. Something the average viewer can relate to, he thought. The reviewers won't be able to accuse me of middle-class cultural bias after this.

"Some afternoons, between showings, I looked round Malkins. Remember that music shop between the pawnbrokers and the tailors in the Old Brompton Road? Nice selection of music and second-hand instruments. One evening there was a violin in the window. Reddish gold body."

His fingers flexed, as if itching to caress the smooth wood.

"I pushes open the door and Mr. Malkin gives me a big smile, and without me saying nothing, takes the violin out of the window and hands it to me. 'E knows, yer see. Knows that instrument was made for me. I checks the fiddle. Bridge well set on the frame, strings nicely angled at the neck. When I tightens the bow, the hair's firm and supple. When I pluck the strings, I know I have to buy this fiddle."

He frowned. "That violin made me old fiddle sound like old Ma Riley on a Saturday night, compared to Caruso." He leant forward, staring Matthew straight in the eyes. "You understand, mate, don't you? It's all very well for toffs to say that a bad workman blames his tools, but..."

"So did you buy it?" Matthew asked eagerly.

Boris wasn't going to be hurried. He sat back and thought for a few seconds.

"An instrument like that's an investment. A smart young fella like you knows all about investments. With a violin like that, I could get a better job, be leader instead of second fiddle. It'd pay for itself in a couple of months, and then we'd be in the money.

Tony was moving up North, and there were three of us after his job. If I had that fiddle, I'd get his place. And that meant more dosh. 'How much?' I asks Mr. Malkin. '£30 — £25 to you,' says he. So I tells him I'll have to talk it over with the missus."

"I goes home. Loretta's expecting our first, money's tight. But she was a grand girl. 'You know best, Boris,' she says. 'I trust you.'"

Matthew watched the joy of possession and hope sweep over Boris' face. Wonderful, he thought. Aspirational. Something every consumer can empathise with.

"Women was like that in them days. They let the man decide. So I get that violin. Couldn't have been happier. The future was bright. I looked for clouds on the horizon but there weren't none."

He stopped talking. The technicians stopped moving. The producer was silent.

Matthew let the silence roll, waiting for the denouement.

"Two weeks later it happened," Boris said at last. "We were down the pub, when Tony comes in, his face white as a sheet, his eyes full of despair. Thought his missus had died or summat, we did. 'Have you lot heard the news?' he asks. His voice sounds different from usual, squeaky, out of tune like. 'Some jerk in America's invented something called the *talkies*.'"

The atmosphere in the studio was tense. Matthew stared at Boris, hypnotised. This was the subplot of his own life. Short term contracts. Labour saving improvements. No security. The constant threat of unemployment.

"We couldn't make out what he was on about. Me and Fred look at him confused, like. Femi calmly swigs his beer and beats a rhythm on the wood of his kora. 'What you talking about, Tone?' says I. 'Park your bum, I'll get in a round.'"

"Tony gulps down his pint. 'This'll change everything,' he yells. 'They're gonna record the actors' speech!' We look at him like he's gone nuts. Fred says, 'What you worrying about them old actors for? They makes enough lolly — they don't need to graft! Rolling in it they are!' 'Don't get it, do you?' shouts Tony."

Boris paused again, milking the tension and the drama. Matthew knew what he was going to say. He fingered his collar, waiting for the inevitable crash.

"Remember like it was yesterday, I do. I put me glass down with a thud. Blood drains from me cheeks. 'He means they're gonna record the music as well as them old actors' voices!' I tells the lads. 'Curtains for us, comrades! No need for pit musicians no more. This new process'll save the film industry millions of dollars. But it's gonna put thousands out of work. Including us!'"

Matthew could picture the scene in the pub as if he was there. He could smell the cigarette smoke, see realisation dawn in the musicians' eyes.

"So what did you do? What happened to you all?"

"Well, lad, same as what happened to them car workers in Dagenham, or the shipbuilders on the Tyne. Same as what always happens when some clever bugger gets a good idea. Out on the streets! Thousands of musicians queuing up for jobs as bus-drivers, mechanics, builders. Fred gets a job as a music teacher, Femi joins a jazz band. I tried for a place in an orchestra, but there was so many of us waiting at the stage door, I never even got a chance to audition!"

Matthew let out his breath in a sympathetic sigh.

"OK, wrap it up," came the message through the headset.

"So Boris, how did you support your family?"

"Well, sonny. The baby was nearly due, the rent had to be paid. Loretta's on about kiddies' clothes and second hand prams."

Boris picked up his imaginary instrument again.

"I plays one last tune on me beautiful violin. Mr. Malkin gives me back me £25, and hangs the fiddle in the window."

He winced. "Funny really. I'd only been on the dole for a couple of weeks when I bumps into Bert. 'How yer doin, mate?' Bert asks. 'Not so good!' says I. 'Unemployed, ain't I? Some dozy geezer's gone and invented the talkies, and lost me me job!' Bert says he's sorry to hear that, and takes me for a pint. Then he asks if I've still got me old tools. Tells me there's a couple of vacancies for sparks down the factory. Reckons there's a war coming, says there's a demand for skilled workers."

Pure Henry James! Matthew thought. A circular story, conflict and resolution. A Film Studies course brought to life. The programme would probably win the next *Film about Films* award.

Warmly shaking Boris' hand, Matthew turned to the camera.

"You've been watching *Life Behind the Screen*. We'll be back next week with our special guest, scriptwriter Lorrie McKenna. Today I was talking to Boris Petulengro, a musician from the era of the silent movies."

Barfield's *Atchin tan*

Although Zula was almost nine, Mam never let her walk to school on her own. That was because Zula's Dad had been murdered. Killed in a brawl, just before Zula was born. If Zula asked questions about him, Mam would cry like a rainstorm. So Zula didn't talk about him any more. All she knew was this. There'd been a gang of skinheads, and skinheads didn't like Travellers.

If Zula's Dad hadn't been killed, they'd have still been travelling with the Fair, instead of living on the Council Estate at the bottom of Barfield Hill. But Mam's heart had been broken so she had to stay near Barfield Hospital for monthly checkups.

Zula was good at guessing when the Fair was about to arrive. She heard distant voices calling her name. She could smell candy-floss on the September winds.

She also knew when someone was about to whisper something nasty about Travellers. Her spine would tingle and a mist would form in front of her eyes. She got that feeling today, on the way to school. People were muttering over garden gates, tutting and shaking their heads.

"Can't trust them dirty Gippos as far as you can throw 'em! Nicked our garden bench last year, they did!"

"We've fetched our garden gnome into the sitting room, just to be on the safe side!"

Mam pulled Zula onwards down Marlow Lane, a hard look in her eye. Zula wanted to tell those old cows where to stuff their stupid gnomes and rotten benches. But she kept quiet. She knew Mam was frightened of making a fuss. Frightened that Zula would get hurt.

If I had a Dad, the neighbours wouldn't say such nasty things, Zula thought. I wish he was here. She clutched Mam's hand and swallowed hard. There was a big lump in her throat, like that time she'd choked on a boiled sweet.

She longed for a big family, like Greta O'Connor or Lilah Lee. But ages ago, back in the war, something had happened in Hungary to most of Mam's Romani relations, something so bad Mam couldn't talk about it. Mam had been born and brought up in Luton. After she married Zula's dad, they travelled with the Fair.

Zula was told off for daydreaming in class three times that day.

"Coming down the Fair later?" Vicky asked her at playtime.

"You bet!" Zula said. "See yer down there."

After school, Mam was waiting in the playground as usual, chatting to Greta's mother, Siobhan. The two women walked slowly down the alley as Vicky, Roberto and Amina chased Zula and Greta down to the main road, where a slow-moving procession of lorries and trailers was juddering along. Impatient motorists hooted, trying to overtake the huge, colourful rides, and the schoolkids cheered and yelled, waving to the truck drivers.

On the first night of the Fair Mam and Zula always took doughnuts to the *atchin tan*. There, on the other side of Marlow Lane, next to the path which ran past

Zula's school, lay a grassy clearing, just big enough for three small caravans. That's where the Lees always camped when they came to Barfield with the Fair. It was their family place, had been for hundreds of years. That's what Uncle Johnny said, anyway.

As they crossed the road, Whacker looked up and whinnied a greeting, and Lilah, Robin, Rowany and Col ran to greet Zula, tugging her into their caravan, showing off badges and postcards from Appleby and Stowe. Mam handed round the doughnuts while Auntie Zeta hooked the kettle over the fire.

Smoke wrapped round Zula like a familiar blanket as she tried to think of something interesting to tell her friends.

"Our school's got a new outdoor swimming pool," she boasted. "Come and see!"

Leading them up the alley, Zula pointed to a gap in the school fence. "See that? On warm evenings, us estate kids slip in there for a swim."

"Come on," called Mam. "Time for me and Auntie Zeta to start work."

Mam had changed into a long orange dress and tied a scarlet scarf round her hair. Auntie Zeta was wearing a shiny green skirt and yellow blouse. Zula grinned at Lilah as they walked with Uncle Johnny and the other children to the common.

"You're so lucky to have such a big family. You must always feel safe."

"You kidding?" Lilah asked. "I'd give anything for the chance to hear meself think! I reckon it's right *kushti* to live in a house and go to school in one place!"

Zula was astonished. "Would you really like to live in a house? It's so lonely and boring!"

"Swap you then!

They turned into St. Albans Field. The condoms and needles that usually littered the field had been cleared away, and the common was covered with booths and rides. The food stall was in its usual spot, with Flora busily wiping the candy-floss machine, and Zak greasing the hamburger griddle. It was as if the Fair had never been away.

"Stella! How you getting on, gel?" shouted Flora as soon as she saw Mam.

"Good to see you!" Mam responded. "Welcome back!"

Uncle Rees had set up a tent in the field, with a big notice outside saying, **YOUR FORTUNE TOLD BY TRUE GYPSIES**. As soon as Auntie Zeta and Mam had disappeared through the canvas flap, Zula ran off with Lilah and Robin, greeting stallholders, hopping on the rides.

She saw her friend Greta staring over at her.

"Hey, Zula," Greta called, looking at Zula's gang. "Can I play?"

"Mam said you're not to talk to them tinkers!" hissed her brother, pulling her away.

"She never did!" yelled Greta. "She likes Zula and her mammy."

Lights from the rides flashed in the dusk, and music blared from amplifiers. A woman staggered across the field in high heels and a tight skirt, eating a charred burger. Rich youngsters from the mansions of Totterhill, council estate kids and Fair children ran round together, screaming on rides, touched with magic.

"Great innit, Zula!" Roberto called across the field. "Dead exciting!"

Zula waved from the Big Wheel. She was the Queen of Barfield Fair. This was her enchanted realm.

"Wikked!" she shouted back. "Laters."

Zak gave her a hot dog and Flora made her a candy-floss. As Zula was sucking the pink sugar off her fingers, Mam and Auntie Zeta came up, their cloth bags bulging with money.

"Time to go home!" Mam said, taking off her scarf and letting the wind ruffle her dark hair. "School tomorrow!"

Zula was shocked.

"I can't go to school! I want to help Auntie Lou set up in the afternoon."

"I'm coming to school with yer tomorrow!" said Lilah. "We'll come down the Fair after."

Next morning, Mam and Zula collected Lilah from the *atchin tan*. "You're turning into a right beauty with them big brown *yoks*," Auntie Lou smiled, tweaking Zula's curls. "Are you *jelling* off with us when we leave?"

Zula looked at her mother, imagining travelling to faraway places. "Can I, Mammie?" she begged.

"When you've got your exams, you can choose!" Mam replied. "When you're older."

Zula frowned. She didn't want to take exams. She didn't want to study. She wanted to be free. Maybe she *would* swap places with Lilah.

Miss Shavani welcomed Lilah to class. "We're going to start making a chart of Romani/English words," she announced. "Zula can help Delilah write some words about food, and the rest of you can draw the pictures."

"Wow!" said Zula, kicking Lilah in delight. "Cool."

At dinner break, Tom ran up to Lilah and slapped her arm. "Dirty Gippo!" he shouted.

Zula whacked him on the head, and Tom ran off snivelling.

After school, Miss Shavani went into the playground, looking for Mam. "You're gonna get it now!" sneered Tom. "Serves you right for belting me!"

But the teacher only wanted to ask Mam to accompany a class visit to the Fair.

Next day, excited pupils from Marlow Lane School straggled down to the fairground where Auntie Lou was waiting for them. "Hello, children," she said. "Anyone want to look round?"

"Yes!" roared the class, frightening the birds from the trees.

When the children had seen all the rides, Uncle Rees handed out free toffee apples.

"Cor, ace, innit?" exclaimed Tom, face smeared with syrup. "Wish my dad was a Gippo and worked in the Fair! He only works in Waitrose, all we ever get are horrible broken biscuits."

Zula felt proud to know the Lees, to be part of the Fair community. When she grew up she'd follow them. She'd run the toffee apple stall, make loads of money, and send Mam to a private doctor.

It happened one humid evening down the *atchin tan*, just before the Fair was due to leave. Auntie Lou was slicing potatoes, while Mam and Auntie Zeta danced to Johnny's violin.

"Let's have a dip in the pool," Lilah whispered. Squeezing through the hole in the fence, the girls jumped into the water, splashed around, then flopped on the warm stone surround in their damp clothes.

"Come on, *chavies*, time to eat," called Auntie Lou from the little encampment.

Zula chased Lilah back to the *atchin tan* for fried potatoes and sweet tea. Pete brought out his accordion and Mam danced a few more steps, only stopping when she started to cough.

Despite the food she'd just eaten, there was an emptiness in Zula's stomach. This is the last night we'll spend together till next year, she thought. The violin played a mournful refrain, full of anguish and smoke and longing.

Suddenly she heard a childish scream. Whacker neighed and the dogs started barking. Pete ran up the alley and peered through the fence. "There's a *rakli* in the pool!" he yelled.

He pulled the girl from the water and carried her back to the fire. Auntie Zeta massaged the child's chest till the girl choked and started to retch.

"That's Greta! Greta O'Connor!" Zula shouted.

"Better get her up the hospital!" said Mam anxiously. "I'll phone Siobhan on the way."

Johnny backed the cart into the road and Mam climbed up, cradling Greta in her arms

Zula's heart thudded uncomfortably. It was her fault. She'd nearly killed Greta, her best friend. Greta must have been hanging around, wanting to play. If only I'd seen her, she thought. I'd have let her play with us.

Wiping away tears, she stared at the cold stars, praying Greta wouldn't die.

Everyone sat miserably round the *yog*, waiting for news. After a long time they heard Whacker's hooves clopping back along the tarmac road. The hollow sound reminded Zula of a vampire film she'd watched at Vicky's house. The part when the monster hammered nails into the coffin.

"They've kept her in," called Johnny. "She'll be alright, but it's a bad do! They'll blame us Fair folk, for sure."

"They will that," agreed Auntie Lou.

Next morning on her way to school, Zula saw

policemen swarming over the *atchin tan.*

"Them Gippos drowned three kids last night!" Roberto said in the playground.

"Shut your mouth, stupid *gorjer*!" Zula screamed, blood pumping in her temples.

Miss Shavani took her hand. "Come along, class. Mrs. Martinez has called an assembly."

The excited buzz in the hall died away as the headmistress came in looking cross. Her voice was cold and firm.

"Greta O'Connor nearly drowned last night. She's in hospital, but luckily she'll be all right. I'll be sending out letters reminding your parents that no one's allowed to use the pool unsupervised."

Zula stared at the floor. She knew Mrs. Martinez was looking at her.

"It was them Gippos," Vicki said as they filed out. "Tried to murder Greta O'Connor."

"No they never, you filthy liar!" yelled Zula. "My uncle saved her!"

Miss Shavani gave them one of her looks.

All through the lesson, Zula was weighed down by a heavy load. She knew she'd never escape from the taunts and the jibes.

At playtime there were muffled whispers. "Murderers, they eat babies."

"They're thieves, they kidnap children!"

A thin warm hand pressed Zula's arm. Turning, she saw Amina.

"They talk such crap!" Amina laughed. "They reckon us Somalis eat kids too! You can play with me and Fatima!"

The Lees were packed, ready to leave. "Come with us, Stella," Auntie Zeta begged.

Mam's face was full of sadness. "I can't. You know I have to stay near the hospital. I'd not survive a month on the road."

Zula's heart ached as the caravans lurched down the narrow path to the main road.

The *Barfield Tribune* printed a photo of Uncle Bobby with his arm round Greta O'Connor, beneath the caption

BARFIELD GIRL SAVED BY TRAVELLER.

Miss Shavani pinned the article on the board next to the word chart. "Zula's uncle is a hero!" she said. "If he hadn't jumped into the water, Greta would have drowned."

At playtime Roberto bit off some chewing gum, offering a damp grey pellet to Zula. She punched his hand away and ran off with Amina.

The next edition of the *Tribune* featured a reader's indignant letter.

"The Gypsies nearly drowned a Barfield child! How much longer must we put up with such behaviour? The Council must act now!"

Mam tutted and threw the paper in the bin.

During autumn half-term, Mam and Siobhan took Zula and Greta to Jennyburgers in Barfield town. On the way home, the girls raced down the alley leading to Marlow Lane.

"Wow! Will ye look at that!" Greta cried, as they ran past their school.

Zula gaped in surprise. Last week there'd been a small meadow with room for three caravans to pull in. But the little *atchin tan* had disappeared. Instead, an enormous flowerbed spread across the grass, enclosed by concrete bollards and low walls, with scarlet chrysanthemums covering the freshly turned earth.

Giggling, Zula and Greta picked handfuls of flowers and ran back to their mothers. "Aren't they grand!" exclaimed Siobhan.

Zula handed Mam her bouquet, smiling as her mother hugged her. "They're beautiful!" Mam said. "Where did you get them?"

When Zula pointed to the newly erected flowerbed, Mam's smile slowly changed to a frown. She gasped and muttered something.

"Are you alright, darlin'?" asked Siobhan. Throwing down the flowers, Mam grabbed Zula's hand and tugged her across the busy main road.

"Mammie, what's the matter?" cried Zula. Mam didn't answer until they were home and the door safely locked behind them.

"The flowers are pretty, *kamali shay*," she panted, "but you shouldn't have taken them! Don't you see? The Council haven't built that flowerbed for the people of Barfield! They've done it to take away the *atchin tan*! Auntie Zeta and the others won't be able to stop there now. The Council have ditched up their camping place!"

Coughing, she covered her mouth with her hands. Zula stared at her mother, trying to understand.

After a long silence, Mam looked up. Her face was strained and there were tears in her black eyes.

"That's not a flowerbed, it's a graveyard! Our Lees won't be able to camp there any more. The Council don't want Traveller sites in the borough, they're trying to drive us off."

Zula shivered.

Autumn had turned into winter.

The fire had gone out.

The Lady Who
Turned into a Card

A scarlet wheel on a blue and green flag, bright against the grey sky.

Gisela leaned against the stone balustrade, tired after the journey from Oakton. She'd forgotten how hectic London was, and wondered how she'd ever managed to cope with the daily commute from the suburbs.

But she was glad she'd come. Glad she'd brought Andrej. It was important for her young son to know his roots.

At Victoria Station, Andrej had taken charge, carving a path through the hurrying passengers. As they walked along the Thames, past the London Eye, the sun had come out and Gisela had started to feel happy. Like a tourist. Not like an Asylum Seeker. But by the time they approached Blackfriars Bridge, clouds were sweeping across the river and sorrow pressed down on her again.

As more people clustered round the banner, Gisela recognised students and lecturers from the South London University she used to attend. Orfan and Lynne waved at her, and Thomas came over and hugged her warmly. She felt comforted and valued as they talked of past conferences, the latest statistics on Gypsy sites, the paper she was due to present to the United Nations.

"Going to Istanbul next week?" Donald asked.

"If I can get funding," Gisela replied. But she knew she wouldn't go. The twenty minute trip from Oakton had exhausted her. It was an effort to socialise with her old teachers, and pretend she was still that angry young refugee, the fiery student who was going to avenge a dreadful wrong. No way could she present an academic paper or formulate eloquent phrases. She couldn't talk about it all again, it made no difference anyway.

She had to think of Andrej. She couldn't allow herself to be torn apart.

At last the procession moved off, marching over the bridge. Thomas had brought a huge box of mixed blooms, irises and roses, tulips and daffodils. Orfan and Jozef carried the banner. When they reached the middle of the bridge, everyone stopped to throw flowers into the water below.

The wind, gusting wildly, blew the flowers back on the pavement. Andrej laughed as tulips and spring daffodils fell into the path of passing cars and lorries.

"Why you do this?" a puzzled Japanese tourist asked, squinting at the banner. "It say Roma. You are Football Support Club?"

"It's Roma Nation Day," Thomas explained. "April 8th. People all over the world gather to honour the Roma Nation and celebrate Gypsy culture. We throw flowers into rivers."

"Hai, hai! I see!" The tourist smiled blankly, gave a slight bow, and started videoing the banner.

There were speeches outside the Houses of Parliament. Gisela strained to hear what Orfan was saying, but the wind gushed his words into the sky. She caught snatches of sentences — unfair media representation, stereotypical images, awareness raising, shifts and ruptures.

She closed her eyes. She'd heard it all before. The words didn't put out fires or bring corpses back to life.

"Gisela! Are you OK?" asked a familiar voice.

Gisela looked up. Liz, her social worker from the Refugee Welfare Commission, was standing next to her, smiling sympathetically.

"Oh, hello, Liz. I am OK, thank you," Gisela replied wearily. "And you, you are OK also?"

"You look really pale," Liz said, opening her eyes wide and puckering her brow. Gisela smiled uncertainly. She knew Liz was signalling her willingness to listen and help, but the middle of Blackfriars Bridge during a Roma Nation Day rally wasn't the time or place for a discussion.

Andrej was talking to Lynne and Donald, throwing back his head and laughing. When the wind ruffled his black hair, he looked so like his father, Gisela's heart lurched and she swayed, feeling faint.

Liz took her arm. "Come and have some lunch. We're off to a workers' caff round the corner — I'll treat you."

Gisela followed Liz to the cafe and sank into a chair. Andrej was already there, tucking into a plate of sausages and chips.

"Are the pills helping?" Liz asked in her clear voice. "Dr. Feld's an expert in trauma stress conditions. I'm so glad he was able to take you on."

Gisela nodded, reluctant to discuss her medication in public. Liz ordered coffee and sandwiches, and turned back to Gisela.

"And you're happy with the new accommodation?"

"It is very lovely," Gisela told her. "It is very good

for Andrej to have his own room. And we like the garden very well."

Liz squeezed Gisela's hand. "That's marvellous! I'm glad you came today. I was going to phone — I've managed to get a grant to buy you a multi-channel television. The Refugee Commission will pay the bills. I argued that you need cable TV for study and research purposes."

Gisela smiled. Sometimes she found Liz intrusive and insensitive, but other times she was surprised by her thoughtfulness and support.

"Thank you so much," she said. "Andrej will be pleased, he is complaining always about our old TV."

When the new television system was installed a few days later, it took up half the wall in the sitting room. Liz called round to make sure Gisela knew how to operate the complicated machinery, and expertly pressed knobs and buttons, slipping DVDs into slots, pointing the remote control at the screen.

"Thank you," Gisela said, looking at the huge shiny equipment. She found it an effort to speak, and had to force out the words. "I thank you, Liz, for the lovely house. Thank you very much for the television. It is all very beautiful."

"No problem." Liz stood up. "It's my job. Don't forget to ring if you need help or advice. Or if you just want to talk. It's good to talk."

Sometimes the past is too difficult to remember, Gisela thought, showing her visitor to the door.

While she was clearing the cups from the sitting room, her eyes were drawn to the large, grey screen. The cold empty space seemed to be staring at her. Picking up the remote, Gisela started to flick between channels. Westerns, a Turkish programme,

BBC news, samba dancers, football, a girl belting out a pop song.

She went into the kitchen and mixed minced lamb, onions and green peppers in a bowl, adding flour, eggs, and herbs. She rolled the stiff mass into sausage shapes and poured oil into the pan she'd been given by the Refugee Welfare Commission.

I'm a beggar, she thought. I who studied so hard, with two degrees from Prague University, now living in a rented cottage paid for by charity. A cottage stuffed full of furniture donated by kindly strangers.

She prepared a salad, put the food in the fridge, and went back to the sitting room. She checked the television again, switching from channel to channel in the hope of finding something to watch.

How many programmes can there be, she wondered. So much choice, so much rubbish. She pressed the remote listlessly.

That's when she found the card channel.

It was fronted by an attractive auburn-haired woman in a grey silk suit with stylish silver studs in her ears. Her co-presenter was a middle-aged man with a kind face and a calm authorative manner. He reminded Gisela of Professor Stefka from the Prague Faculty of Sociology.

The woman looked lovingly at the man as he talked. Perhaps they're married, Gisela thought.

She realised that the woman, Meriel, was demonstrating how to make cards. As she talked, Piers, the man, held up examples.

"We'll be showing you how to make cards for all occasions," Meriel said. She spoke so slowly that Gisela understood nearly every word. "Cards for weddings, for baptisms, for Ramadan, Chinese New Year, Christmas, Chanukah, Diwali, barmitzvahs, birthdays, and naming ceremonies. Cards for funerals and newborn babies. Thank you cards. Congratulation cards for passing exams and driving tests. Have I left anything out, Piers?"

Piers adjusted his yellow bow tie. "I don't think so, Meriel. But I'm sure the viewers will email us if we have."

They hadn't mentioned cards for the murder of a husband. But there probably wasn't much of a market for that. Not in Britain.

"Over the next few weeks we'll be telling you how to make these beautiful cards. Cards you'll be proud to give your friends. A personal statement of love and affection."

For the first time since she'd arrived in England, Gisela felt a flicker of excitement.

"I'll make cards," she told the figures on the screen. "I'll go out with Andrej tonight when he gets back from school, and buy what I need. Tomorrow I'll start making cards. I'll make a Thankyou card to give to Liz. I'll sell cards to local shops, at fairs and fetes, in markets, to friends."

But she had no friends in England. Apart from Liz, and Liz was a social worker and didn't really count. Liz was paid to be her friend. Gisela cried as she remembered Ema, Vilma, Marusha and Pavlina. Such dear companions, thousands of miles away.

She made a cup of tea, and swallowed two of the pink pills prescribed by Dr. Feld.

Usually she woke tired and had to force herself out of bed. But next morning she rose early and made a big breakfast. Andrej's eyes lit up when he saw the table set with plates of eggs, cheese and bacon.

"You feeling better, Mama? Are your tablets working at last?"

"I'm feeling better, my dear."

As soon as her son left for school, Gisela washed the dishes and turned on the television. Meriel was there, with nicely made-up eyes and a fresh hairstyle. Piers was in the same suit he had worn the previous day, with a green bow tie. The presenters smiled. They showed the type of glossy paper and trimmings needed for festive occasion cards.

Gisela opened the packet of coloured card and the bag of braid she'd bought the previous day, laying adhesive glue and sharp scissors on a tray.

"For birthday cards, you need a theme," Meriel explained. "A special hobby, or a favourite place, for example. Let's take Piers, for instance..."

"Oh, yes please!" Piers grinned at the camera.

"He likes golf and opera. So I could choose a picture of a golf club, or a character from *Aida*. I make a rough sketch of the object and cut out the paper shape. Then I stick it on the card."

Miraculously, a beautifully designed card featuring a golfer appeared on screen, with a greeting written in bold sweeping italics.

Andrej likes the accordion, thought Gisela. His accordion was destroyed in the fire, like everything else. Bora had just started teaching him to play. He said Andrej had a real feel for the instrument. If I sell enough cards, I'll be able to buy him a new one, he can have lessons.

The first accordion she drew looked like a fan, the second like a radiator, but then she folded some red paper over and over, producing a passable image. Selecting green card for the background, she stuck the accordion shape on top.

It didn't look very professional, but it was acceptable. "I don't suppose you made your card yourself," she said to Meriel. "I bet you had a team of designers and artists to help."

She hid the card in her dressing table drawer, ready for Andrej's birthday in November.

Now the presenters were showing a selection of knives. Stanley knives, delicate craft knives, and a circular blade that could be rolled over paper to cut out swirling shapes.

Piers held up a beautiful paper rose with fragile petals and stamen.

"Isn't that a work of art!" exclaimed Meriel, fluttering her eyelashes. "If you want to design delicate flowers or scroll patterns, sharp blades are an essential part of your kit. You can obtain them by mail order from …"

Gisela turned down the sound and went into the kitchen. She couldn't look at the knives. Knives took her back there, to the old Czechoslovakia, somewhere she didn't want to go, could never, would never think about.

Sometimes the fatigue was so heavy, she couldn't bear its weight.

Swallowing her midday tablets, she made a cup of coffee, taking it back to the sitting room. Piers and Meriel were still speaking soundlessly, and Gisela giggled, startling herself with the sound of laughter.

Turning up the volume, she realised the presenters were now discussing the merits of various coloured papers. "Rainbow Products do a spectrum of tones ranging through the chromatic register. The sheets are good quality, and excellent value."

Piers held out a fan of coloured sheets, while Meriel talked the viewers through the endless possibilities.

"Black provides a dramatic background, or can be

used for silhouettes."

The camera zoomed in to show three examples. Gisela looked at the cards in admiration, and practised cutting out slivers of paper with her new scissors as the website address of Rainbow Products flashed up.

Letting her hand move freely, she drew an abstract squiggle, slit through the oblong of black card, and pressed down. Holding the rectangle up to the window, she stared through the empty shape. It looked like the flames of a fire. She placed a sheet of orange paper behind the black stencil, and the flames flashed into life, vivid and sharp.

When Gisela had been a child, fires were a joyful sign of feasts and festivals. Like in springtime when Roma would come from other villages and towns, setting up camp on the hillside or by the river. Each family lit a small fire, and jumped over the flames. It looked like the hill and river were burning.

Not long after she'd moved to Oakton, she'd seen her next-door neighbours jumping over a tiny bonfire in their back yard. "They must be Roma too!" she exclaimed to Andrej. "But they've got the date wrong. They should jump in May, not March."

It was Andrej who suggested taking them round some cakes. "You'll be able to talk to them, Mama. It will be good for you to have some friends. I've made friends at school, but you've got no one."

Children always tell the truth, Gisela had thought, and while Andrej completed his maths worksheet, she cooked *langushe* with cream cheese to take to the neighbours.

Just as she pushed open the gate of the neighbour's house in the morning, a woman in a headscarf came out wheeling a pram, talking to the baby in a language Gisela didn't recognise. The woman looked at Gisela in alarm and scuttled back into the house.

Later Gisela discovered that the woman was from Iran, and that in Iran, people jumped over fires at their New Year in March.

She glanced at the clock. Half past three. Time to clear up the paper and glue.

"Hey, Mom, what's for tea?" Andrej slung his backpack on the sofa and slouched in front of the TV. Taking the remote, he switched to the football channel.

Over the weeks, Gisela's stack of cards grew. The cards were stored in drawers, in boxes on top of the wardrobe, and under the bed. As soon as Andrej went to school, Gisela switched on the television and made cards with Meriel and Piers.

The charming couple were her new friends, her family. They were slicing through the fog of despair that had swirled around her for so long.

One day, they showed the technique of colour layering. Meriel, her fingers covered in expensive silver rings, demonstrated how to stick layers of different coloured card together, then slice diagonally through the sheets so each colour was visible.

Gisela sketched out a design and opened her art box, selecting three sheets of card — red, gold and brown. Following Meriel's instructions, she stuck the layers together. Red for blood, gold for the sun, brown for the earth. Leaving the adhesive to dry, she went into the kitchen to put the chicken in the oven and slice potatoes into a baking tin.

She swallowed her tablets with a biscuit and some mint tea. Then she washed and dried the drinking glass thoroughly, taking it into the sitting room where Meriel was still chattering away.

Upending the glass on the card she'd prepared earlier, Gisela drew round the rim with a pencil, forming a perfect circle. She snipped away with the sharp blades of the scissors, smiling as the colours were revealed.

Next, she drew round a five pence piece. A hub. She traced sixteen thin oval shapes so they radiated outwards. Once more she sliced through the thick card, forming the spokes of a wheel. She stuck strips of blue and green paper on a backing sheet. Her hand was getting stiff; she flexed her wrist and concentrated on the television.

The presenters were now advising their audience about the best kinds of braiding and ribbon.

"Satin adds lustre and gloss," Meriel told her. Gisela wasn't sure what lustre and gloss were, but guessed it was something to do with the sheen of the material.

"I had a satin dress when I was a girl," Gisela sighed. "It was for my sister's wedding. Everyone said I looked beautiful."

She closed her eyes. The dress, like everything else, had gone.

"And chiffon allows transparency and light to shine through..." Meriel continued.

Gisela studied the shape she'd cut out. It looked good. A crimson cartwheel layered with gold and brown. A shakra, a prayer wheel. The image on the Roma Nation flag.

Picking up the cut out wheel, she bored a hole through the centre of the hub with a needle. Then she skewered the wheel to the backing sheet with a pin. She flicked the wheel with her fingernail, making it spin.

The colours blurred as the circle whirled round, sucking her into the vortex, into the centre. She became a symbol. A wheel.

I am the wheel that turns, the wheel that rolls, the wheel that crushes, the wheel that kills.

She was pinned to the card, spinning giddily in an endless round. The wheel wouldn't stop. The shape devoured her.

The doorbell rang.

Gisela gasped, breathed hard, and wrenched herself back from the spinning wheel.

Holding onto the walls for support, she made her way dizzily to the front hall. Opening the door a crack, she saw her neighbour. The woman was crying and holding out a screaming red-faced baby.

"No spik England!"

Gisela ran to the bathroom with the child in her arms, followed by the wailing mother. Wetting a flannel, she placed the damp cloth on the baby's forehead, massaging its hands and stomach, whispering rhythmically. Gradually, the child stopped screaming.

"Doctor!" she told the mother. "You go to doctor."

"No England. My man no." The woman shook her head and mimed a man forbidding his wife to speak to the English.

Gisela mixed vinegar and honey in a glass of water. She dripped some of the liquid into the infant's mouth, poured the rest into a clean jar, and screwed on the top.

"Give baby three drops morning and night," she said.

"*Merçi!*" The woman struggled to find the English word. "Ta, mite."

"Name?"

"Maryam. You?"

"Gisela. Coffee?"

Gisela moved to the kitchen, ready to light the gas. The woman hesitated. "Man no like me England."

Gisela laughed. "I am not England. Have coffee."

"*Merçi. Kheili mamnum*! Ta, mite."

I should thank you, Gisela thought. You saved me. I almost turned into a card. For the last few months I've sought refuge in my cards, lost myself with Meriel and Piers, forgetting who I really am. If you hadn't rung the bell...

That night, when Andrej was in bed, Gisela took up the report she'd begun writing the year before.

"In much of Central and Eastern Europe, since the collapse of Communism, the Roma have been vilified, marginalised and persecuted. Many have been killed. My husband, Jozka Bora Mittale, was dragged from our family home by seven skinheads. He was tortured, mutilated, and murdered. Our house was burnt. All our possessions were destroyed, and my son and I were forced to seek asylum in Great Britain. I demand United Nations protection for my people, as set out under the Bill of Rights. I demand recognition and compensation for the atrocities committed against us."

She printed out the statement and folded it neatly, using the sharp creases Meriel and Piers had taught her. Just before closing the envelope, she had an afterthought.

Taking the card she'd made that afternoon, the card that had almost swallowed her, she attached it to the report.

"Let the wheel roll," she said.

The Land of Swans

A ray of sunlight, deflected by the glass swan mobile, dribbled onto the pillow.

Oleg opened his eyes, smiling as prisms splashed over the duvet cover and the sleeves of his cygnet patterned pyjamas. Still half-asleep, he stretched out to catch the glittering feathers of light.

There was a rap at the door. "Are you up, dear?" Linda called. "I'm just off to wake the others. Back in five."

Oleg fumbled in his pillowcase and drew out his secret supply of Swan and Edgar matchboxes. Selecting one, he sniffed its sandy edge, breathing the sulphur deep into his lungs. Clumsily, he twisted the yellow box and looked at the picture of the white swan on the green lake, rubbing his fingers over the scratchy scraper and the bird's smooth wings.

Very slowly, he sat up, swinging his feet down onto the swan-embroidered mat. The matchbox fell to the floor.

There was another knock at the door and Linda bustled in, smelling of soap and cheap perfume. "OK, Oleg? Let's get you to the bathroom and give you a shave."

Oleg liked Linda, although she said his name in a funny way and looked like a duck with her stubby hair. Following her to the sink he asked, "Linda, have you got a swan?"

He shut his eyes as the care assistant washed his face and rubbed it dry. "You and your swans!" she laughed, scudding the electric shaver across his cheeks. "Haven't you got enough? Those old matchboxes take up more than half your wardrobe already!"

Oleg sat silently on the bed as Linda buttoned up his shirt and eased the trousers over his stiff legs. Even Linda didn't understand. Nobody did. He looked at the wall, at the swan picture he'd painted last week. People were always asking him why he wanted another swan, but he couldn't explain. All he knew was that each new bird filled the black hole in his heart, momentarily easing the pain.

When Linda bent to lace up his shoes, Oleg wanted to stroke her hair. But he didn't. He knew he'd get into trouble if he touched her. That was something called "inappropriate behaviour." If someone did "inappropriate behaviour," they weren't allowed to go to the cinema, or have sweets, or visit the pub with the volunteers.

Linda stood up. "Come on, love, let's get you down to breakfast. If you're good, I might be able to find you another matchbox."

It was noisy in the dining room. Zahid had spilled coffee on the floor and Eileen was screaming. Oleg drank tea and ate cornflakes, staring at the matchbox, lost in his private myth.

"It's a swan," he murmured. "It's a swan."

When Debby ran past shouting, Oleg thrust the swan into his shirt pocket. He always tried to keep away from Debby. Debby was dangerous. She liked to snatch his matchboxes and throw them out of the window. Last time she did that, Oleg had gone into the grounds to find his swan. He'd sat on the grass waiting for it to fly back.

He'd waited and waited, and then he'd begun to walk to the green lake. After a while he got tired and sat under a tree, watching the stars come out. Later some people in uniforms came in a car and brought him back to the Home.

Everyone had shouted at him. Even Linda had been cross. But the next morning, she'd given him another swan matchbox.

Oleg finished his toast. It was time to follow Linda up the stairs to do his teeth. When he'd sucked the minty paste from the toothbrush, Linda helped him into his coat and took him out to the minivan. "Bye, now," she said, patting his arm. "That's me done till tomorrow."

She slipped a slim yellow matchbox into his hand. Oleg was so pleased he didn't mind that Mfon was on escort duty today. Mfon was always grumpy and in a rush. Mfon pushed him into a seat, buckling his seatbelt with an angry click. He waited while the others squeezed into their places and were fastened in.

As Tony the driver idled down the road, Oleg began to relax. This was the best part of the day. The van passed through villages with pubs and churches. Some of the country pubs had pictures of swans — black or white or gold — hanging from signs that swung in the wind.

Sometimes they passed buses with swan logos painted on the sides. And sometimes, on magic days, they passed a lake with a real swan swimming on the shiny surface. That would make Oleg remember the night his mother had flown away.

It had happened like this. Once upon a time, Oleg had been young and happy, and lived with his parents and his brothers and sister in a big caravan. Mama was beautiful, with a long white neck, and Papa was kind and strong. His parents were swans who flew high in the air. They leapt from a flimsy wooden swing attached to the dome of a huge tent. The swing was called a trapeze and the tent was called The Big Top.

Papa wore a white suit with glittering stripes. Mama wore a silver dress, which floated round her body like wings as she flew in the air. When the audience clapped and said, "Aah!" and "Oooh!", Oleg was very proud.

There were always lots of circus children to play with, like Marina and Alex, whose father was the lion tamer. Sometimes Marina put her fingers in the lion cub's mouth. Then there was Daniella, the daughter of the bareback rider. She used to canter round the ring in the daytime, learning new tricks. Jojo, Anna and Lara were the children of Koko the clown. Sometimes Koko let Oleg join him in the ring during the performance, and Oleg always got the most laughs.

But this story had come to an end.

At first, he'd thought his father was showing off a new trick. Instead of flying from one trapeze to the other, Papa had done this exciting stunt.

The drums had rolled in a crashing swirl of sound and faded away. Papa balanced on the trapeze and saluted the audience. Then he dived from the ceiling to the floor. It was brilliant. Magnificent. His shimmering spotlighted body twisted and turned, landing in the ring in a cloud of dust and sand.

The "Oohs!" and "Aahs!" turned into screams. The band stopped playing.

Papa got put in a box and the box was put in the

ground. A lot of visitors came to cry and eat round the grave. They were dressed like circus people, in long skirts like Mama, or black hats like Papa. They sung nice songs, and played violins. Koko said they were Gypsies too, who worked in other big tops.

Mama said Papa had gone to live in Heaven, up in the sky. Oleg thought this was odd. Papa was in the earth, not in the sky, but people were always saying things that were very strange.

After that, some men in grey suits came and said everyone who worked in the circus had to go away. Back to their own country. Back to the land of swans. Oleg didn't understand. There was a lot of pushing and shouting, just like in the care home when Zahid or Debby did "inappropriate behaviour."

Suddenly Oleg was alone. That's when he first met Linda. Linda had shown him a picture of an enormous silver swan, and said his mother had flown away, back to Romania, where there weren't facilities for young people like him.

"OK, everyone! Here we are!" Mfon opened the van door and helped her charges climb out. Oleg watched as his mates slowly filed into the day centre like a line of parading elephants.

He was alone in the van, sniffing the sulphur on the matchbox, looking at the picture.

"Come on, Oleg!" Mfon shouted impatiently. "Why are you always last?"

Oleg showed Mfon his new picture. "Look, it's a swan!" he said, trying to cheer her up.

"Get a move on!" she snapped. "Get inside!"

Oleg limped into the centre, anxiously clutching his matchbox. Looking round for a friendly face, he saw Dick hurrying down the corridor with an armful of files.

"Dick, look at my picture."

"Not now, Oleg, I'm busy. Got a meeting. That's not another swan, is it? I don't know where you get them all from!"

Oleg sat in the lounge, waiting for the morning activities to begin. He wondered if Kari was coming today. Kari always asked Oleg and Zahid to help carry her big box into the hall. Inside the box there were drums, wooden xylophones, triangles and clappers. Kari ran the music group. Oleg liked Kari, but he didn't like the music. It wasn't proper music. There were no accordions, no trumpets, no violins. No *Oom pah pah*.

The swan on the matchbox cover fluttered its wings. Oleg brought the picture up to his eye, trying to capture the image.

Maybe it was art day. Art was his favourite session. He always painted the same picture, over and over again. Sometimes the helpers said, "That's nice, Oleg, what is it?" and sometimes they rolled their eyes and laughed.

But Oleg didn't mind. He knew that if he kept dreaming, kept collecting pictures, kept drawing long-necked white birds, one day the silver swan would bring Mama back, and she'd take him home.

A Vardo in the British Museum

Nigel Dench was out to make a good impression. The British Museum was full of bright, ambitious people jockeying for position, and he was one of them. As part of the Project Development Group, he needed a novel idea, something that would make Sir Giles sit up and take notice.

His brief was to widen the museum client base and appeal to members of the wider community. Like poor people. Asylum seekers. Youth. Ethnic minorities. As Sir Giles put it, these days it was all about targets and diversity.

Nigel's secretary, Samantha, had listed some websites, underlining those most likely to prove useful. The first one she'd marked was ARTISTS WITHOUT FRONTIERS. Nigel typed the details in the searchbox and clicked GO.

"Can't expect to be lucky first time," he said to himself, waiting for the download. When the grainy images appeared, he noticed that the homepage was too big for the screen, with headings disappearing into the grey computer frame, making it difficult to read. The information had obviously been written by someone whose first language wasn't English, and there were too many tiny icons.

Squinting, he read a couple of items. One was

about a music school in Tashkent. Another described literary evenings in Iran. There were quite a few articles about Iran, he realised, deciding to give the site a miss. The British Museum already had a wide range of Persian exhibits, and he needed to find something really unusual to impress Sir Giles.

But before closing the page, an impulse made him click on the right-hand arrow at the bottom of the screen. This action dragged the word **MAGAZINE** from the hidden zone. A photo appeared. A photo of a young man standing in front of a caravan, under the caption, **ONLINE INTERVIEW WITH JAKE BOWERS.**

Intrigued, Nigel started to read.

Journalist Jake Bowers is proud of his Romani heritage. And he believes that the British Government, instead of reviling and marginalising Romani people in the UK, should celebrate the massive contribution made by this long established minority. That's why he set up the Gypsy Media Company, with the aim of raising the profile of a much maligned community. Jake answers a few questions below.

Brushing back his hair, Nigel leaned towards the screen. He sensed he was on to something. Something big. Something revolutionary.

Can you tell me a bit about your background? Where did you spend your childhood?

I'm an English Romanichal from the south of England, but I spent my childhood mainly in Sussex, Hampshire and Surrey. I grew up when it was becoming increasingly difficult to lead a nomadic lifestyle. I've lived in every kind of accommodation, from bender tents, to static mobile homes, caravans and council accommodation, in a period when more and more travelling Romanies were being forcibly settled on municipal caravan sites or driven off the road by changing economics. I was born into a world radically different from that of my parents and grandparents, at a time when the Gypsies' usefulness to the British countryside was diminishing, and our presence was no longer tolerated.

Nigel was surprised. This Jake Bowers claimed to be a journalist, but Gypsies were supposed to be illiterate. The guy probably writes for one of the tabloids, he thought. Like *The Sun*. Then he remembered there'd been some fuss about headlines in *The Sun* not long ago. So maybe not *The Sun*. A hack for the *Daily Mirror*, then.

Nigel buzzed through to his secretary.

"Samantha, when you've got a minute, can you find out what *Romanichal* means? I know what a Romani is, but not sure about *chal*. Thanks."

He continued to read.

When did you start the Gypsy Media Company? What are the aims of this organisation?

I set it up in September 2003. The aim is to improve the representation of Gypsy people, whether in the arts, the media, heritage institutions, academic research or in the services provided to us. We are the only media production company in the UK owned for and by Gypsies themselves. We are a social enterprise based on the principle that if you want to know the truth about a community, you must ask the only real experts: the community itself.

Check out — <u>www.thegypsymediacompany.co.uk</u>

Nice one, Nigel thought, pleased by the mention of heritage institutions. I'll invite this Jake to write a piece about the British Museum in *The Mirror*, encouraging Gypsies to visit us. Sir Giles will like that.

He scribbled down Jake's website address for future reference, wondering what exhibits might be of interest to a Gypsy visitor. Perhaps the Viking section — Gypsies liked fighting and brawling. Then there were the golden artefacts of Roman Britain — everyone knew Travellers liked bright colours and bling. Or the Indian section. Gypsies *were* originally from India, after all.

You started a British Romani radio station. Who are your audience, what language do you broadcast in, and what issues do you cover?

The target audience is primarily the Romani community in the UK. But there is also a secondary audience of *Gadji* (non-Gypsy) people, who are either interested in our situation and culture or who simply stumble across the station. We broadcast in English, but also use the station to increase knowledge of Anglo-Romani. We look at community issues, such as health, education and most importantly, access to secure accommodation, as well as dealing with softer subjects like culture, whether that's music, dance, arts or even comedy!

"Clever chap, this Bowers!" Nigel muttered to himself. "I'll definitely contact him, get him to publicise the British Museum on his radio show. Free advertising's the way to go, get one over the opposition. I'll have to act quickly though, before the Museum of London gets wind of my idea."

As Nigel scanned the screen, the word *museums* leapt out at him, and he read to the end of the interview with growing excitement.

I'm particularly interested in your work with museums, promoting the much neglected contribution of the Romani community to British life. How have regional museums and their visitors reacted to this innovation? Do you envisage high profile museums like the British Museum following suit?

There is an urgent need for our history and culture to be recognised and included with British mainstream heritage work. Knowledge of the past has a direct impact on perceptions of the present. I'm convinced that working with museums and libraries will have a real impact on how Gypsies are treated. If nothing else it will nail the myth that we are "invaders" of Britain's green and pleasant land. After all, we were a crucial part of the rural economy long before many former city dwellers saw their first hedgerow. And I won't stop making that point until there is a palatial, ornate Romani *vardo* (wagon) alongside every other national treasure in the British Museum.

Nigel shouted with delight. "That's it! Just what I've been looking for!"

He switched on the intercom. "Samantha, please come in. The very first website you suggested is perfect. Drop what you're doing and bring your dictaphone. We need to make plans."

Six months later, Nigel hosted the launch party of the British Museum Romani Artefacts Gallery. Sir Giles shook his hand warmly, talking about great opportunities for a young man of such vision.

Nigel led the dignitaries and journalists on a tour of the exhibition, smiling as the visitors admired the examples of Gypsy crafts, the horse trappings hanging from walls, the tinning and woodturning equipment clearly displayed with explanatory notes and diagrams. Installed around the hall were huge archive photographs of Gypsies working the land.

Pride of place had been given to the old caravan Samantha had tracked down, its carved edging newly repainted red and gold. Nigel had prepared a speech about his admiration for Romanichals and his commitment to their cause. His closing line read, "I am so pleased to welcome Gypsies and Travellers into our historic museum, and look forward to forging links with you all."

As Nigel waited for Sir Giles to call out his name, he imagined the congratulations the culture correspondents from *The Guardian* and *The Times* would shower on him. And of course, after his inspirational words, he'd be invited to appear on *The South Bank Show* and *Newsnight Review*.

But to Nigel's surprise and disappointment, he wasn't asked to speak. Instead, Sir Giles led Jake Bowers to the front of the room and asked him to open the exhibition.

Jake stood in front of the caravan, running his hand over the ornate wooden frame, looking just like he did in his online photo.

"It's been my dream to see Gypsy culture take its

rightful place in institutions celebrating British history and culture. I'd like to thank Sir Giles and Nigel Dench for making this possible."

Jake was silent for a moment, staring into the distance. When he spoke again, his voice echoed round the room.

"This is a great day for my people. A recognition of our worth. At last, there's a *vardo* in the British Museum."

The Mermaid

Sand beneath her fingers. Grit in her eyes. Pebbles under her cheek. Salt on her lips.

Cold. Wet. Stiff.

A wave washes onto the shore. She closes her lids again, and sleeps.

She wakes to a shroud of clean sheets and the smell of disinfectant. Faces, different colours, like shells, sway above her.

Someone bends, whispers in her ear. Music, spray flying off the sea. She smiles. The sound is lovely. "Whatssssssssssssssssssssss. Where. Who." The sound dies away, like a sighing wind.

Bread. White bread. Soft. A nurse breaks the bread into small pieces, and pokes it into her mouth. She swallows and chokes. The nurse pats her back until she stops coughing.

"Whatsssssssssssssssssssssssssssss," the nurse says.

She shuts her eyes again, sinks back into the safety of the dark.

Soup. Pureed fruit. Bread. Water. Fresh water.

A dress, several sizes too large, slips over her head and is zipped up. The nurse takes her arm, guides her down a corridor.

The corridor sways and she clings to the nurse's arm. Giddy. A chair. A cup of tea.

More faces. "What's your name? Where are you from?"

She doesn't understand the words.

Strangers huddle round, staring as if she's a new species of life. A man is pushed forward.

"Bonjour Madame. Comment vous appelez-vous? D'où venez-vous?"

She closes her eyes. Behind her lids everything is calm and peaceful, splashes of colour lighting the darkness.

A nurse holds the cup of tea to her lips. She swallows. Time waves past, in eddies and billows.

Meat and gravy. A cup of coffee. More voices calling her in.

"Digame! ¿Como se llama usted, querida? ¿De donde viene?"

"Wie hiessen Sie?"

She doesn't know where she is. She doesn't know who she is. Questions have no meaning for her. She is warm and dry and cared for. Safe.

The nurses start to call her Mermaid. She doesn't know what it means, but looks up when she hears the sound.

One day a different sort of man comes to look. A dangerous man. A dark suit man, with a grey tie and pale blue eyes. When he sits beside her, words float out of his mouth.

"What's your name? Do you speak English? Where are you from? How did you get here? Who is your next of kin?"

She has now heard these words so many times before, she can repeat them in her head.

"We can't keep her here for ever!" the man tells the doctor. "Apart from her reluctance or inability to speak, there's nothing wrong with her. This is a Psychiatric Unit, not a hotel! Get the media involved. Someone must recognise her!"

Mermaid knows he's cross. She looks at his shiny brown shoes. Lace up shoes. Shoes that can kick and stamp.

Next day, they dress her in jeans and a black blouse, and carefully brush her hair. Her lips are dabbed with pink gloss. The nurse takes her into an office. There's a man with a camera, and a lady with a dictaphone.

The lady smiles and asks the familiar questions. Mermaid understands, but cannot answer.

The man pushes her head into various positions. The camera flashes. Sun dancing off the sea.

She sinks down in the chair, burrowing into the cushion. The man and woman leave. A volunteer leads her into the garden. The sun is shining, the sky is blue. She smiles.

"Mermaid, who are you?" the volunteer asks. "*Min ismish?*" The volunteer has black hair and dark eyes. She looks familiar.

Mermaid stretches out her hand. The volunteer touches her finger and offers her some chocolate.

A word starts to form deep in Mermaid's stomach. It rises slowly, out of the depths, turns into a gasp. She presses the volunteer's hand, comforted by its warmth.

Midnight. The moon hangs in the window like a lantern. Something is calling her, drawing her to the lounge. She gets out of bed and blindly walks into the large, shabby dayroom with its rows of orthopaedic chairs. She goes straight to the ancient black Steinway in the corner. It's like a ship, caught on rocks.

Fumbling with the lid, she holds her breath, but the piano isn't locked. She sits down on the stool.

Waves crash on the shore, over cliffs, dashing spray

and seaweed into the air. Lightning flashes, thunder roars, the ship falls and rises, tossed by the sea.

When the storm ends, her hands rest on the browning ivory keys.

The noise of pebbles falling on a beach. She turns. Nurses and pyjamaed patients are standing behind her, yawning and clapping.

That night she dreams. There was somewhere, not here, not now. There was a man who smelt of horses and of hay. There was a woman who smelt of mint and lemon. There were children laughing and singing. The woman, a mother perhaps, cleaning classrooms in an old school. A piano. There was a child, a barefoot girl fingering the keys at night, while the mother swept and scrubbed. A child making beautiful songs.

As she grows stronger, more people come to talk. Different words, same questions.

"*Kak vas zavut? Ot kuda vi?*"

"*Tamarun naam shun che?*"

And the word in the deep begins to gather strength and shape.

One morning, when they ask her their questions, the word flies out of her throat, like a seagull flying to the sun.

"Rom..." She stops. She senses danger. She closes her mouth.

That afternoon, they bring a young man with golden skin and a friendly smile.

"*Buon giorno, senora. Como si chiama? Di dove lei? Italiana? Da Roma?*"

"*Roma!*" she agrees. Her throat aches with the effort. Her vocal chords tremble with the strain. When was the last time she spoke?

Her visitor begins to talk quickly, laughing and

spreading out his arms. *"Roma,"* he repeats. *"Roma."*

The man in the brown sweater, the one who always speaks to himself, is banging idly on the piano keys. He stands up and bows when Mermaid goes over, as if to acknowledge the piano belongs to her. When she plays, long roads stretch before her, green hills, warm summer rain, violins and birds.

"Says she's from Rome," one patient tells another. "Eyetai."

The man in the brown sweater stops mumbling, and starts up the Tarantella song. *"La la lala, la la lala, la la lalalalala ...."*

His voice, though harsh, is in tune.

Mermaid catches up the melody, dives into the music. Nurses and patients link arms, swinging round and round in the dance.

A cleaner pats her arm, smiles, clucks. One of the patients, Mebel, she thinks her name is, comes over and gives her a hug.

Mebel takes Mermaid to one of the urine-stained chairs. She smoothes Mermaid's dress. The volunteer with the dark eyes combs Mermaid's hair.

Sometimes, Mermaid helps in the kitchen. She loads the dishwasher, cleans the stove. It reminds her of the ship.

Why was she on a ship? Where did the ship come from? Where was it going? She doesn't know.

Where is she now? What is she doing here?

The questions torment her. The piano calls her, and she sits down to play. The music seethes, soothes, bubbles.

"Look!" It's the nurse called Femi. She's holding out a newspaper, pointing at the front page.

There's a picture of a woman with braided hair and

staring eyes. Above the picture is some big black writing. Femi reads it out.

Mermaid's hands crash down on the keys.

A ship appears on the horizon of her memory. A band. A piano. Friends. A small cabin. Laughter. Warm arms. A sailor. She plays clouds and thunder, a body falling from a high deck. As her fingers pummel the keys, the man in the brown sweater starts to weep.

It's summer. When she walks outside, the flash of a camera makes her jump. Journalists are hiding in the grounds. She freezes.

They come closer, calling, "Mermaid, who are you? Mermaid, where are you from?"

Crouching to hide from their hungry eyes, she sees a small hole in the hedge which separates the hospital from surrounding woodland. Mermaid slips off her clumpy trainers and lets the earth and grass push against her feet. Squeezing through the gap, she runs down a forest path. She stops to listen but no one is following.

She leans against a tree. Warmth from the rough

bark seeps into her skin. Insects buzz past, golden in shafts of light. A little bird hops nearer, chirping.

Two children come out of a clearing, twigs in their hands.

"Hello!" they greet her. "How you getting on? Are you coming to visit?

The little girl pulls Mermaid along. "We're wooding," the child says. "You can help."

Mermaid knows this dance. Bending, stretching, selecting dry branches, stacking them in piles. Silently she works with the children.

"Look, Ma," the boy shouts as they near a huddle of wagons. "We found a *rawnie*. Sitting by a tree. Don't say nothing though."

"Why, I reckons that's the woman wot they was talking about down the pub!" says a man with a scarf knotted round his neck. "*Dicked* 'er photo in the paper."

"They said she come from Rome. Italian, they reckons. Look at her face, though. The spit of our Rosie. Could be one of us."

Mermaid is sitting in a large trailer, holding a cup of tea sweetened with condensed milk. She runs her fingers over the fine porcelain, smiles.

"Don't you worry, gal," says one of the women. "You can *atch* with us. We'll look after you. You stay as long as you like."

Her new friends start to talk very quickly. Incomprehensible words swim round her, till one jumps out like a flying fish. The word *piano*. One of the men rummages behind a curtain. There's a squeak and the sound of bellows.

"We ain't got no piano, *pen*, but have a go on this."

An accordion is placed in her arms. Mermaid slips the worn leather straps over her arms, adjusting the buckles so the instrument sits easily on her lap.

Energy pours into her fingers. She begins to play. A prayer, an incantation, a dirge, an elegy, a butterfly, a ship, a seething sea, loneliness and love. Loss and redemption. Playing up a storm.

Atch Poggering Mandi

If he didn't move, he could bear the pain. Just. If he didn't breathe.

Air forced itself between his dry lips, into his lungs, squeezing acid along his ribs.

Words thundered through his head. *Atch poggering mandi*. He tried to scream them out, but they stuck to his tongue.

Stop bullying me!

Sam wanted to bring his right hand up to his face, but it was numb. He couldn't feel his fingers.

There was a snorting in his ear. Something wet on his cheek.

"What you got there, Rex?" he heard someone say. A man's voice. Kind. "Found a nice bone?"

Sam tried to speak, but nothing came out of his mouth.

"Jesus! Keep still, lad! Don't move."

A rough hand prodded him, checked his pulse.

"You'll be OK, boy. What's your name?"

"Sam." The sound was like a groan.

"OK, Sam, you're going to be alright."

There was a rustling sound and something was placed over his body. A jacket. The fabric smelt of mud and sweat. The weight of it pressed on his bruised chest.

A familiar noise above his head. A number being

keyed into a mobile phone. The dog licking his hair.

"Ambulance. Back of Richards Hill School, in the woods. Young lad, about ten or eleven I'd say. Found him lying on the ground. In a bad way. Been beaten up, I reckon."

There was a click as the man squatted beside him. Same noise Dad's knees made when he knelt down.

"Ambulance is on its way. About fifteen minutes they reckon. You be alright till then? I'll stay with you, don't worry."

"Thanks." The word wheezed out like a busted harmonica.

"OK, lad, don't talk. Just lie there. Got a right going over, didn't yer? Must have upset someone pretty bad."

There was a metallic clank and the crackle of paper. Sam knew that noise. Opening the baccy tin. Thumbing out tobacco shreds. Making a rollup, like Grandpa.

The scrape of a match. The cigarette smoke seared through his nose, making him cough.

"Hey up, boy, take it easy, now." The man brought his face closer, and Sam squinted up at him. The man had smiling blue eyes and a brown beard.

"Where d' yer live?" the man asked.

Sam moaned as a hot wave of nausea washed over him. He closed his eyes again.

"Sit, Rex!" the man commanded the dog. "The boy don't want you slobbering all over his face."

Rex scuffed the grass, turned round three times, and flopped down, tail thumping.

"You rest now, I'll do the talking. Name's Greg. Live in the village, have done all me life, and the parents before me. Grand place it is, friendly, or so it was till the newcomers moved in. Now it's all second homes and commuters. Sort of split the village into newcomers and locals, different now."

Sam liked listening to stories, and willed the man to go on.

"They're the ones stirring up all the fuss about them Gypsies. Tell yer the truth, I don't give a monkey's who lives in that old meadow. Not been used for years, not since Ma Jilly Fletcher died. But the newcomers, always organising meetings and contacting the papers and what have you. Say they don't want no Gypsy kids in school, disrupting lessons."

An insect ran over Sam's neck. The sky swirled in a dizzy pattern of gold and grey clouds. Liquid trickled from his mouth.

"Load of nonsense, I call it," Greg continued. "Live and let live, I say. We've allus had Gypsies round here, I tells them. Part of the countryside. Used to help at harvest time, come back again with the horses in spring. Never had no trouble with them before."

Greg made a sudden movement, and Sam guessed he'd flicked the cigarette stub away. Rex stood up, thumped his tail, and licked Sam's arm.

Greg pushed the dog away. "Ambulance should be here soon. Feeling any better, son? Wanna tell me what happened?"

The sky had stopped turning. If he breathed very gently, a whisper came out of his throat.

"Big boys. Bullies. Gippo, they called me. Dirty Gippo. Get out of our school. Leave us in peace."

He shut his eyes. He could see it all, like a film. Nigel grabbing his schoolbag. The bag spinning into the bushes. Josh kicking him to the ground. Others, he didn't know who, stamping on his body. Laughter. Girls jeering. *Pikey. Gippo.*

"That's how it was, eh?" the man said. "Thought it must have been sommat like that. Well, we'll see about that, lad. Got laws nowadays. I'm only a simple working man, but I know what's right. We'll get the police onto it. Ain't that school of yours got anti-bullying rules?"

An accordion was being squeezed in Sam's head. Two notes, louder and louder. Sound of an engine thundering across the woodland trail.

"OK, sonny, you're alright, we've got you."

He was in his own episode of *Casualty*. Paramedics strapped him to a stretcher, placed an oxygen mask over his swollen face.

"Can I come with him?" the man asked.

"Sorry, sir, we can't allow your dog inside the ambulance."

"Make sure they know it was school bullies what done that to 'im."

When Sam woke, his mother and father were sitting by his bed. "O *dordie*, I thought you was dead!" Mam screamed. "Whatever have they done to you?"

Cautiously, Sam lifted his head. There was a plaster cast on his right arm, and bandaging on his body.

"You're going to be alright," Dad assured him. "Broken arm, and a cracked rib. You'll be up and about within the week, you'll see."

Briony and Billy ran down the ward. "Are you better?" Billy asked, bouncing on the bed.

Sam groaned as pain jerked through his chest.

"Leave off!" Dad pulled Billy onto his knee. "Your brother needs his rest."

"There was a man," Sam lisped through swollen lips. "Greg. He helped me..."

Mum leaned over and smoothed his hair.

"The police want to talk to you. Mind you tell them what happened. Ambulance man said you was bullied."

"Told you not to send him to school," Dad said. "Look at the state of him. Half *mullered* he is."

"I've got some friends in class," Sam choked out "Owen and Hamid and Kate."

Back in his bed, in the trailer. Kids playing outside. Dogs barking.

A knock at the door. Mum talking to a man. His man, Greg. A woman's voice too.

"Me and Maggie, the wife, thought we'd drop by to see how you're doing." Greg smiled, holding out a comic and a bag of sweets. "Been up the school, I have, had a word to that headmaster of yours. Told him how you looked when I found you. Things'll be different now. They got them thugs what done you in. Nasty pieces of work. Couple of them newcomers' lads, but one of them a village kid, I'm sorry to say."

"Will you take a cup of tea?" Mum asked.

"We will that, Missus, if it's no trouble."

"Thank you," Sam said to Greg. "Thanks for staying with me."

Greg shrugged. "You're alright, lad. Glad to help. Now I got a bit of a suggestion. I run the local boxing club. How about coming down for a few lessons?"

Sam shook his head. "I don't like fighting."

"He's a quiet one, our Sam," said Mum, "Always got his head in a book. Our scholar, we calls him. Writes letters for us, too."

Maggie laughed. "No reason why Sam can't keep on reading. Our lad Ed, he's a great reader too, but he's learnt to defend himself. Used to get bullied, but no one'll touch him now. Keeps him out of trouble, down at the club three nights a week. Our daughter goes as well, says it's not fair to have one law for boys and another for girls."

Sam flicked the pages of the comic with his left hand. There was a drawing of a fat boy punching in the head of a little lad. Behind him stood a skinny child about to land a kick on the bully's fat bum. KERPLAP. The bully went flying and the little kid was saved.

Sam lay back. He'd think about it. He wished everyone would just leave him alone.

Stop bullying me, he thought. *Atch poggering mandi!*

Tea?

Nobody ever looks at her. She's only the tea lady. She comes in at eight-thirty in the morning, an hour before the first session, and collects up the dirty cups left by evening-class students. The mugs are always jumbled untidily over the draining board and the counter, one or two stranded on the small tables at the back of the canteen. Some are lipstick stained, a few have cigarette butts floating in them, some are smeared with traces of chocolate or biscuit crumbs.

The tea lady puts on the yellow rubber gloves provided by North Finchley Community College, and fills the blue plastic bowl with hot water and suds. She watches the foamy water rising up the sides of the bowl, then plunges the cups into the liquid. She wipes the smooth china mugs with a sponge, rinses them under the running tap, places them on the rack. She imagines she's rescuing victims from a shipwreck and bringing them to safety.

At eight forty-five, the first student arrives. The tea lady doesn't need to turn round, she recognises Reza by his sigh and his footsteps. He comes early as he has to vacate the Whetstone Hostel for Asylum Seekers after breakfast. In Iran he taught in a High School, now he works evening shifts in a pizza parlour for £5.50 an hour.

Reza sits in the corner of the canteen to do his homework, clutching his pen painfully as he forces it to move from left to right across the page. His dark hair falls across his face, he pauses and looks unseeingly past the tea lady.

The tea lady takes a clean towel from the drawer and starts wiping up. She works quickly and carefully, stacking cups on a chipped wooden tray.

Murmuring a soft greeting, Merouille from the Congo pushes through the swing door and sits in the corner opposite Reza, stretching out her long legs. She stares into the distance. The tea lady has heard that all Merouille's family were slaughtered. Merouille is young and pretty and sad. Her skin glows under the glare of the harsh light.

The tea lady fills and switches on the urn. More students arrive, shivering with cold, pulling thin coats tight around them, hitching up saris, adjusting shalwar kameezes, shaking rain from umbrellas. The tea lady knows all their names. She sees the students every day.

"Hazer e?" *"Water hot?"* *"Il y'a du thé?"* *"Chai gotovo?"* *"You chai ma?"* The words begin their daily whirl, dancing before her.

She shakes her head. "Soon!" She continues putting out the cups, checking the money in the float, wiping down the counter, arranging catering-size tins of teabags, coffee and drinking chocolate, getting large cartons of orange and apple juice from the fridge. She pours milk into a green jug, watching the creamy liquid foam. A drop splashes onto the laminated counter, she wipes it with her cloth, and checks the urn.

The first wisp of steam lifts the metal lid. The tea lady tenses. The water is ready. Instinctively, the students turn and crowd round the counter. It's nine o'clock. There are about twenty students in the canteen now, gossiping, laughing, recounting humiliations. *"Wo gan mao le!"* *"c'était hier, à cinq heures,"* *"fuimos a Londres..."* *"mard kheili bad bud."* They jostle and push each other good-naturedly. When they get to the counter, they stop talking to their friends and force their jaws into unaccustomed shapes, frowning with the effort.

"Vun cup of tea pelis." Abdullah from Kosovo produces his sentence like a symphony, each consonant separate.

"Pliz give me wun kup tea," Mei Li says in a breathy tonal rush. Merouille asks for coffee in her French Congolese accent, carefully counting out the money. She carries her mug back to her table and sits silently with a friend.

The queue grows longer, the tea lady pours and serves, smiles and serves. Tea, coffee, juice, chocolate. Empty cups are returned as the students start to leave the canteen. It's nine-thirty, time for class. The tea lady walks round the canteen, collecting stray mugs stained with lipstick, smeared with chocolate. Refilling the bowl with hot water, she washes the mugs, dries and stacks them. She works quickly, she has to be finished by nine forty-five today, because the Poetry Group is holding its first meeting in the canteen. The tea lady has been told to take a break during the session so the group won't be disturbed by the clatter of cups.

The tea lady drapes the wet dishcloth over the urn to dry, and sits down by the sink behind the counter, flexing her aching back. She glances over the counter dividing her from the rest of the canteen, and sees some new students come shyly into the canteen. They sit awkwardly at separate tables. Quick confident footsteps tap along the corridor, a tall pale woman in a brown suit and long flowing scarf enters the canteen, carrying a file.

"Good morning, everyone. I'm Ruth, your facilitator. This poetry group is to help you express yourselves in English. Most of you have written poetry in your own country. Our college has been awarded a grant by the Arts Council to publish some of your poems, to raise awareness in the wider community and to raise money for equipment for our students." Ruth smiles, words flow smoothly from her mouth. The poets stare at her, trying to understand.

"Let's start by moving our chairs into the centre of the room so we're in a circle." The poets reluctantly get up and place their seats in a ring. "I'm sorry we can't meet in a proper classroom," Ruth apologises. "But this is the only available space, and at least you'll be first in the tea queue at break!"

She laughs and looks round expectantly. No one else laughs. Someone drops a pencil, somebody rips a page from a writing pad.

"Now I want you to tell me about yourselves. Your name, where you come from, what you do. I'll start off. I was born in England, but my parents were exiled from Germany during the Second World War, political refugees like you. I've had two volumes of poetry published." She places two slim books on the table. "These are my books, you may want to look at them after class."

The participants reluctantly mumble their names, looking at the floor. Fowzia from Iran, Batchu from Bangladesh, Ferdi from Nigeria, Murcia from Bolivia, Din Yun from China, Valbona from Kosovo, Fatima from Afghanistan and Huma from Algeria.

Behind the urn, the tea lady listens to their stories.

"My family was killed by Serbs," Valbona is saying. "But my best friend, a Serb, hid me in her garden shed and helped get me over the border. If it wasn't for her... I don't know if she's still alive, they have perhaps killed her for helping me, an Albanian."

Huma adjusts her headscarf. "My brother was imprisoned for speaking out in Algeria. I started a campaign to free him and they tried to arrest me. Ahmed's still in jail, I escaped and came to England."

"I refused to wear a *burkah*!" Fatimah shakes her thick dark hair. "I did not want to become invisible. I taught girls in secret but someone told the Taliban and I had to leave my country."

Din Yun twists in her chair. "I was arrested after the uprising in Tiananmen Square. I ran away and hid, then some friends brought me to England in a truck. But my boyfriend, my brother too..."

Din Yun bursts into tears. Fatimah gets up and puts her arms around her. There's a long silence, then Ruth clears her throat.

"Well!" she says brightly. "Let's hear the last few stories, and then we'll do some writing exercises."

Quietly the tea lady leans forward to switch on the urn, and settles back in her seat. The sad stories are burning her head, a curtain of smoke hangs over her. Batchu was tortured in Bangladesh. Ferdi's wife was killed by government soldiers. Murcia wrote poems attacking the system in Bolivia. Fowzia distributed leaflets in the streets of Tehran.

"Now we all know a bit about each other," Ruth says, "I'd like you to think about your first day in England. What was it like to come to a different country, to find customs you didn't know — hear a language you didn't understand? How did you get here? Work in small groups, in twos or threes."

The students start talking amongst them-selves, eagerly comparing impressions of the firm, incomprehensible officials who interrogated them at Heathrow, the confusion, the relief, the sadness of leaving their homelands.

The urn begins to drone, emitting faint wisps of steam.

Ruth suggests adjectives, gives examples of alliteration, asks the poets to write down ideas. The students scribble, suck the ends of pencils, scratch their heads, look in dictionaries, ask Ruth for help.

"I need a word for feeling sad, when something you have no more is missing," says Fatima.

"Nostalgia?" suggests Ruth.

When Fatima smiles, her curls bubble round her face.

"There is a word like criminal, but is not that. It means when you cannot get a job because you are foreign."

"Oh, you mean discrimination."

Batchu repeats the word. "Yes, discrimination."

His hand closes round the pen; he etches the new word onto the page.

"I want you to work on your poems at home," says Ruth. "I'll collect them in after a few weeks and the best poet will win one of my books."

The students look pleased. Ruth glances at her watch. It's nearly teatime The urn is boiling, the water humming softly inside the metal container. The tea lady stands up, ready for the rush.

The canteen rings with disjointed sentences as students from the language classes come in for their break. They need to liberate their tongues, relax their mouths from the tyranny of Anglo-Saxon. *"Nada de eso, chica!" "Wo bu dong." "Le prof a mal expliqué." "Urok ochen trudno."*

The term passes in a rush of cups and images, tea

towels and onomatopoeia. Every afternoon at three o'clock the tea lady takes off her overall, draws the rubber gloves from her slim fingers, pushes back her hair, and gets her coat from her locker. She walks down the street to her bedsit. Sometimes she looks out of the window at the small patch of sky above her room, sometimes she reads or writes. She goes to Friern Park Library and uses the computer, she surfs the net. She has no friends, she doesn't speak to anyone. She gets a ready cooked meal from the shop next door, or a takeaway from Reza's pizza parlour near Tally Ho Corner, to warm in her tiny oven.

It's nearly the closing date for the Poetry Competition. Ruth tells the class to title their poems and type them out in the IT session. "But don't put your name on your work," she says. "I don't want to know who has written the poem, so my judging will be completely fair. I'll collect them in next week."

The following Tuesday, the students hand Ruth their poems. She puts the work in a file. When Batchu kisses his poem before giving it in, a ripple of laughter spreads through the canteen. The tea lady smiles too. At break the poets queue for drinks and the tutor leaves the file on the table while she fetches the register from the staff room. The file is still on the table when the tea lady collects the cups. She fingers it with her rubber gloves, wondering whose poem will win.

It's nearly the end of term. Decorations for Diwali and Christmas stretch across the ceiling and a foil star hangs above the urn. *Salaam, hale shoma? Ni hao, ni hao ma? Salut, ça va? Keif ahalek? Kem cho? Nasilsin? Hola! Zdrastvi, kak ti?* The sounds whirlpool round the tea lady till the students disperse to their classes and the poets arrange chairs in a circle, waiting for Ruth.

The tea lady wipes the last cup, spreads the damp dishcloth over the urn, and sits in her usual place. She wants to hear the poems. She wonders who has won. She thinks it will be Ferdi, his poems are deep and sensitive, they make her remember things that have been submerged for years.

Ruth bustles in with her file and her smile. She greets the group and sits in her usual place. Opening the folder, she takes out a sheet of paper. The students stir expectantly, hopefully. Murcia gives a nervous cough.

"All your poems were excellent," Ruth assures them, "but the undoubted winner is the one I'm going to read out." There's a collective sigh, the students look at the ground to hide their impatience and their longing.

Ruth takes a deep breath, smooths back her hair. As she begins to read, the tea lady's scalp prickles, she sits very still.

We run westwards in the wind
guided by the brightest star,
the star my father gave me.
"Look, Esma, look!
There is your star, shining in the night."

Blood red roads
of flames
and screams
smoulder along
the border.
"Look, Esma, look!
There is your star, gleaming in the sky!"

Following the star to the sea,
we drift, we dream,
a teacup in a storm
lashed splashed
by waves
washed up and over.
"Look, Esma, look!
"There is your star, glowing in the sky!"

Fished,
ropeladdered to safety,
big men in a big boat
rinse us, dry us,
bring tea with milk and sugar.
Soft shadows float around my ears,
bitter bubbles burst my mouth.
"Look, Esma, look!
There is your star, glittering in the sky."

On land, a pale sun
a paper cutout -
a ghostly face,
a uniform
asks questions.
I live, I lived in a village which is no more,
which has vanished like wind on waves.
I speak Romanian, Hungarian, French, English,
My mother tongue is Romanes.
"Look, Esma, look!
How your star glistens in the darkness."

I am the water girl.
You do not see me.
You do not know me.
I studied at the University of Bucharest,

The students stare at each other, trying to discover the identity of the winner. They look round enquiringly, but no one claims the prize, no one is grinning shyly, no one is waving their hands dismissively to show their unworthiness.

Ruth clears her throat. "This poem has all the elements I wanted, honesty, imagery, resonance. Come on now, who's the lucky winner?"

Nobody stirs. "Don't be shy! The writer should be very proud of him or herself."

No one answers. Then as the silence becomes uncomfortable, palpable, beating in their ears, Fatima says, "It is not me."

"It is not me, too!" echoes Murcia. Each student adamantly denies authorship.

Ruth studies the poem carefully. "It's strange, I don't understand. If it wasn't any of you, who could it be? This is very bizarre!" She gazes round the canteen, puzzled.

The tea lady is sitting in her usual place, her dark hair hidden beneath the white cap which throws shadows on her bronze skin. The tea lady's eyes are black pools. Her body is shrouded in the white overall issued weekly by the College Catering Department.

"You?" asks the tutor.

The tea lady feels the veil fall from her face as a current flows between her and the tutor. She wants to say, "I was a doctor. I was a poet. I recited my poems at festivals in towns and villages in my country. Some of my poems are in books. I wrote about freedom and hope, about equality for my people.

This is my story. They came for us. 'Burn the filthy Gypsies!' they screamed. They dragged my husband from bed. They broke his arms and legs. They torched the house. 'Run, Roma scum, run!' I took my baby and followed my star. My beautiful baby died on the ship. That's why I'm here. That's why I sit behind the border of my counter, safe, invisible."

She looks at Ruth. She tries to smile. She opens her mouth, but only one word comes out.

"Tea?"

Dancing with Angels

They hadn't discussed having a baby, but Serena sensed this might be their last summer of freedom. So she wanted to do something special in the holidays, like visiting Spain to see flamenco dancers.

But Artie said that sounding boring. He fancied going to an ecological village in France.

Eventually a friend gave them a leaflet about a centre in the Highlands that ran courses in July. "Something for everyone," Serena read from the brochure. "Sailing, singing, art, Gaelic, woodcraft, gardening. And look!" Her voice rose with excitement. "They do Balkan Gypsy Dancing."

Serena taught Dancing at the local College. "I'd like to learn more Romani dances," she commented. "This centre sounds perfect. I'll put you down for Gypsy Dancing too, shall I?"

She waited for Artie to protest.

"No way!" he yelled. "I'll do woodcraft — might learn some different techniques. But you're not getting me poncing around!"

They boarded the train at Kings Cross, installing themselves in the sleeping compartment. By the time they reached Newcastle, Artie was snoring, but Serena peered restlessly through the window from the top bunk, watching the moonlit countryside flash by.

As the sun rose over the Scottish hills, she clambered down, washed in the tiny shower cubicle, and fastened her hair in a pony tail.

Artie was still snoring peacefully. Serena ran her hand over his thin sensitive face, down the laughter lines. Gently, she fingered the silver ring in his earlobe until he stirred.

"We'll be there soon, love. I'll meet you in the dining car."

At Forres they looked for a taxi. The station forecourt was deserted, apart from a young woman using the old-fashioned phone booth. The woman was gesticulating wildly and muffled shouts escaped through the heavy red door.

Artie groaned. "I've got an awful feeling she's going to the Centre."

"Just what I was thinking."

Stiff from the long journey, they sat on the sun-baked wall, backpacks beside them. At last the woman vacated the kiosk and Artie moved towards the phone.

The woman barred his way.

"You go to the Centre too?"

Artie hesitated before nodding.

"My mother does not want me to go," the woman announced. "I am Astrid." She jerked out her hand and Artie shook it awkwardly, looking sideways at Serena. "From Denmark."

"I'm going to call a cab," Artie replied, twisting away.

"It is fine. I just now have phoned. First I have called till my mother, and then till a taxi. It soon comes. My mother says I must come home."

"Maybe she's right!" Artie said bluntly.

Astrid sat on the wall, next to Serena. "How old

are you?" she demanded.

"Twenty-four. You?"

"I am nineteen. What course shall you do?"

"Gypsy Dancing."

Astrid fixed her grey eyes on Serena's face.

"You look like a Gypsy. You are a Gypsy?"

"Yes. Both my parents are Romanichals."

"What is this?"

The sun burnt down on Serena's head. The azure sky looked unreal. Stifling a yawn, she replied, "Romanichal — it means a Gypsy from Britain. What course have you signed for?"

Astrid shrugged. "I enrol to do woodcraft, but I think now I shall do Gypsy Dancing with you."

"Good choice!" Artie agreed.

The taxi drove them down the peaceful Highland road, past herds of cattle grazing in lush meadows. As they swung round a bend, the silver line of the sea appeared, gleaming in the sun. Seagulls swooped and white-gold sand dunes stretched into the distance.

"What a lovely place!" exclaimed Serena.

"Aye," the driver nodded. "Ye'll no find a better spot in a' the world. Have ye been to the Centre before?"

Serena shook her head. "We're really looking forward to it. Sounds great."

The taxi driver smiled to himself. "Ye'll enjoy the scenery for sure. Try to get out to the village, it's a bonny place. It's no far."

Turning off the main road, they entered a huge complex of caravans, gardens, chalets and houses. Solar panels glinted on walls.

"Interesting," Artie muttered. "Ecological houses. I had no idea... I might pick up some ideas for work."

"Aye," the driver said. "They're awfie big on

ecology here. Did ye no ken this is a centre for spiritual education and planetary transformation? In the village some say the folks here are a wee bit touched. Mebbe so, but they've brought a lot of good to the area. They let our village bairns attend some courses, my lad learnt African drumming last year. And Kaitleen, that's the wife, she works in the Centre shop. There's no much employment in these parts, ye ken, so we're glad of the money."

As the taxi eased to a halt, Artie fished a note from his pocket and handed it to the driver. The taxi drove off, leaving the new arrivals in the car park with their bags. Overcome by a sense of abandonment, Serena stared uneasily after the departing vehicle.

A little girl with silver hair and a green face appeared. "Hello," she said. "I'm an Alien Princess." Serena looked at Artie and grinned. The girl's hair was covered in tin foil and her face was smothered in makeup. The lurid greasepaint was melting in the hot sunshine, falling in huge blobs on her pink lacy dress.

"I'm away to a Fancy Dress Party. Do you want to come?"

"Yes," said Astrid, picking up her case. The child took Astrid's hand and led her off. Once more Serena felt lonely and isolated. She wanted to run after the little girl.

Artie groaned. "Astrid's just been abducted by ET's sister. This is so weird. Where is everybody?"

"Bizarre," Serena muttered. "That kid probably *is* an Alien Princess — the taxi driver did mention planetary transformation! I think you're right, Artie, we'll never see Astrid again. Her mother'll turn up and we'll be arrested as the last humans to see her! Can you imagine the headlines? Dane kidnapped by

London Gypsies!"

Artie looked at the list of instructions they'd been sent. "Says we have to register in the Community Centre as soon as we arrive."

They wandered around the complex till they came across a workman halfway up a ladder, painting a house. "Summer school visitors are meeting down there," the workman told them, pointing his brush towards a large pentangular structure.

Outside the Community Centre, people were sitting on the grass, surrounded by luggage.

Shrugging off her rucksack, Serena flopped down with a sigh of relief.

"From where do you come?" someone asked.

"London. I'm Serena, this is Artie. You?"

"Doris from Switzerland. *Mein* husband Fritz. We are arriving this morning. We are having a rather peculiar journey. From Basle to Heathrow. Then on the train to Scotland. It is taking us two days to arrive."

"Yes," Serena nodded. "A bit like a pilgrimage."

"*O ja*, this is *zo*. We are coming each year, for the spiritual refreshment and attunement. It is indeed a pilgrimage."

Smoothing down her chiffon dress, Doris gave Serena a beaming smile.

"Flipping heck!" mumbled Artie in Serena's ear. "What have you got us into? It's some kind of mad cult! Have you noticed everyone's smiling? That's not normal! Not in England!"

"We're not *in* England!" Serena reminded him.

Eventually an assistant turned up to allocate accommodation.

"You're in the Guest Lodge," the woman told Serena and Artie, "just on the other side of the green.

Sharing with an Australian and two Swiss guests. You can't miss it, look for the house with the grass roof."

Artie was impressed. "Insulation, right?"

The woman smiled. "Yes, some visitors don't realise that. They think it's very peculiar."

"I'm an architect," Artie explained. "My practice is keen on renewable sources of energy."

The Guest Lodge consisted of several comfortable bedrooms and a spacious lounge. A plump woman was already in the kitchen, making coffee.

"Good day, I'm Irene, from Australia. I'm so overwhelmed to be here again. This your first visit?"

"Yes," Serena answered.

"It's my fifth. I come for the scenery and the wonderful instruction. I'm doing the Gypsy Dance course this time. The teacher, Paula, is marvellous. She exudes music. She's one of those inspirational people sent by the angels to minister to humans."

Irene poured coffee, and Serena coughed, masking Artie's contemptuous snort.

"I'm doing Gypsy Dance too. Do you dance a lot?" She looked at Irene's broad face and stocky frame, at the short thick legs and wide feet encased in heavy boots. She'd found there was always one student in every class who didn't know left from right, who couldn't feel the rhythm. She guessed that would be Irene.

Irene's smile grew broader. "We've got a property in Queensland. I help out on the farm, not much time for dancing. I bet you dance though, you look like a dancer with your slim figure."

Artie glanced at his instructions again. "We'd better get going. There's a group welcome in the Communal Hall at 3.00."

Irene led the way through pine trees and flower lined paths, pointing out places of interest as they went. "See those low buildings over there, that's the Pottery, Weaving Shed, and Art Studio. And right next to the Hall there's a Cafe, open every afternoon."

"It's a bloody communist farm," Artie whispered. "A *kolchoz*!" He started humming *The International* under his breath.

In the dark, cool Communal Hall, a huge candle was flickering in the centre of the room. People were ranged round the candle, balancing awkwardly on large colourful cushions. Irene handed Serena a cushion, and sat beside her, still grinning widely.

A smiling man walked to the middle of the hall. The constant smiles began to irritate Serena, and she fidgeted impatiently.

"Welcome to the opening session of our Summer School. My name's Douglas. I ask you to empty your minds of the troubles of the outside world. Let us tune in."

Immediately, everyone except Serena and Artie held hands, placing their right palm upwards and left palm down.

A hysterical laugh began to form in Serena's stomach. Clenching her abdominal muscles, she bit her lips, her shoulders shaking. She squeezed up her eyes as Irene and Artie grabbed her hands.

"Beaut, isn't it!" Irene whispered. "Always makes me cry too."

"Good," said Douglas. "For the few newcomers who don't know me, I'm the Course Facilitator. I'll help you open your minds to learning and love. May the light of the candle guide us through the darkness of ignorance."

Serena pressed her fingers into Artie's thumb, her hysteria subsiding as she felt the answering pressure from his hand.

"I call on the angels of movement and melody to join us as we dance around the candle."

"I'm not dancing round no poxy candle," Artie mumbled.

The soft strains of a Scottish waltz wafted from a CD player, and Douglas began to pace slowly in time to the music, leading the students in a long winding line around the hall. Serena swayed in rhythm as she walked, trying to ignore Artie as he scuffed his trainers on the floor behind her.

Suddenly there was a cry and the smell of singed cloth. Doris from Switzerland had danced too near the candle, setting the bottom of her floaty skirt alight. Fritz stamped on the hem, Irene ran for water, and Doris calmly assured everyone that she was alright.

"That's a good sign," Douglas said. "It shows the angels have blessed us."

"Wonder if the angels are going to pay for a new skirt!" Artie whispered.

"Now let's tune out," called Douglas.

The participants held hands again, standing in silence for a few seconds. Serena's stomach rumbled. "I'm starving," she muttered to Artie.

"Not surprised, we've not eaten since breakfast on the train!"

Irene, her face fixed in the permanent grin, led them to the Dining Room for the evening meal.

"What do we get? Gruel? Bread and water?" Artie asked.

"No, mate, you get bonza tucker here. Vegetarian, but."

Some people in aprons marched out of the kitchen and placed steaming vats on a large trolley. A woman stepped forward.

"Hello, I'm Helen. I designed this evening's meal. Let's tune in."

Everyone held hands.

Helen closed her eyes. "We give thanks to the earth for this produce. May our food, prepared with love, bring health and strength."

Serena's mouth watered as the lids were lifted off the vats and the smell of rice and roasted aubergine wafted up. "You can take as much as you like," Irene said. "And go back for more."

They piled food on their plates and sat at a large wooden table by the window. More students came to join them.

"I am Anna from Sweden. I come every year here. I do painting."

"Hello. I am Nanneke. From The Netherlands. I am doing gardening."

"My name is Musumi. I am from Japan. I live here, in the community." Musumi leaned forward, her glossy hair sweeping across her childlike face. "The community is very special," she said in almost perfect English. "It brings peace and knowledge to the world. We members have our own houses, but eat communally and spend the evenings together at various entertainments. It is very spiritual."

I was part of a community once, Serena thought sadly. My community was special too.

Forcing a smile, she turned back to Musumi.

"I am eighteen," the young woman was saying. "I will stay for one year and then return home to make a community like this in Japan. The world is very blessed that a place like this exists."

Irene's smile widened. "Too right, dear. Don't know where I'd be without this Centre, that's for sure." She stood up. "Just going to get seconds. I'm really hungry. Can I get you anything?"

Serena and Artie shook their heads.

"Have you seen Astrid?" Serena asked Artie as Irene went to refill her plate.

Artie looked around. "She's not here. I reckon she's gone back to Copenhagen."

After the meal, Douglas called for silence.

"At eight o'clock each night we have Sharing Groups. The leaders are waiting outside to show you where to go."

"What's Sharing Groups?" Artie asked suspiciously. "We don't have to partner swap, do we? Or share clothes?"

Serena was in Petronella's group, Artie was with Douglas. Serena was relieved. She needed a break from her husband's jokes.

"I'm with Petronella too," Irene told her. "I asked to be with her. She's a wonderful leader. You'll love her."

Petronella, a small smiling Brazilian, led her group to a small annexe. She lit a candle, asking everyone to hold hands. "Now let's share our thoughts."

During the uncomfortable silence, Serena stared at the floor. Her only thought was wondering when they were going to do some Balkan Gypsy Dancing.

Nobody spoke. Everyone kept their eyes on the carpet, until a young woman nervously cleared her throat. "I am Karin. I come from Belgium. I feel very privileged to be here."

Petronella nodded and smiled at a middle-aged couple.

"We are Olga and Helmut from Germany. We also,

we feel both very special to be in so wonderful a place."

"I just love it here," gushed Irene. "I love you all. And I'm so happy to see Petronella again."

Petronella looked at Serena.

A gate clanged across Serena's mouth. Sharing thoughts wasn't what she did. Thoughts were private, only to be disclosed to close family. "Don't ever tell outsiders more than they need to know," her mother had often warned her. And although Serena was no longer that skinny child from the caravan site, she still couldn't tell strangers her feelings.

Karin looked at Serena encouragingly. In the ghastly silence, Serena couldn't think of anything to say. Finally, she muttered, "I've come up from London. I'm looking forward to doing dancing and walking by the sea."

When Serena got back to the grass-roofed lodge, she found Artie lying down in their room. "I had to get out," he groaned. "They're completely insane. Douglas gave us something called angel cards with words like LOVE and PEACE on them. You had to say what the words made you feel. I couldn't think of anything, so I said I had a headache, and came back here."

Serena laughed. "Tell me about it! I made a fool of myself too. Anyway, we'll have a great time at the dance tonight. Irene says the band's really good, she's got all their CDs."

The music had already started by the time they arrived at the Hall. The band was playing Serena's favourite tune, and grabbing Artie's hand, she pulled him into the line of dancers.

"Brilliant," she said as the last notes died away.

"Nice music," Artie agreed. They clapped enthusiastically, the sound of their applause echoing round the hall, banging against the walls. Surprised, Serena noticed that all the other dancers had turned to face the musicians and were waggling their hands in the air.

"We do that so as not to scare away the spirits of music with noise," Irene explained kindly.

"Told you they're all mental!" Artie muttered. "We're the only sane ones here."

Next morning, after breakfast, Artie went off to his woodwork group accompanied by Fritz. "I'll probably come back with a totem pole," he scoffed.

"O no, we make ze box for ze angel cards," Fritz told him earnestly. Artie rolled his eyes in horror.

Serena walked to the Hall with Irene, breathing in the pine scented air.

"Here, have one of these," said Irene, opening a packet of biscuits. "I'm still hungry, aren't you? It's this Scottish air."

A figure appeared from behind a tree, smiling warmly. It was Astrid. "Hey, Serena!" she called. "You should come with me yesterday. We made a nice party. We eat jelly and icecream. I learn some Scottish dancing."

"Great!" Serena replied. "We wondered where you'd got to." She shook her head, trying to rid herself of the Alice in Wonderland sensation.

Paula, tall with long dark hair, was checking the sound system in the Communal Hall. The lesson began with a warmup, which developed into a simple routine. Serena quickly picked up the moves, but Irene kept tripping over, apologising nervously to Astrid who was next to her in line. At one point, instead of turning right, Irene kept going to the left and stamped on Astrid's foot.

"My God, she cripples me!" Astrid screeched, hobbling to a seat. "You cannot dance! Go away! You are a danger to this group!"

Flushing, Irene clapped her hands to her sweaty cheeks, and Paula called a short break. When the lesson started again, Irene wasn't there.

"I'm so clumsy," Irene wept in the Sharing Session that afternoon. "I wish I was graceful like Serena. All I want to do is dance, but I never get it right."

Petronella nodded. Embarrassed, Serena handed Irene a tissue from the box on the table. She tried to imagine what it must be like to be so heavy and stiff.

Petronella just sat there, moving her head up and down.

"I thought you did well," Serena said. "You just need to practice a little every day. I dance all the time, you see."

Irene wept even louder. "I'm a clumsy fat *gallah*!"

Petronella smiled and nodded.

"Where's Fixed Smile?" asked Artie at the evening meal.

Serena glanced round.

"She was really upset before, maybe she's gone for a walk. It's obvious there's something wrong with her. I'd love to find out what's underneath that nailed-on grin!"

There was a workshop of Bulgarian singing after supper, followed by coffee and cakes in the cafe.

In the evening, Serena checked Irene's room. Empty.

"I'm going out," she said to Artie. "I'll see if I can find her. I'm a bit worried..."

Outside the lodge, she paused for a second, then went towards the Pottery. On the main path she noticed traces of heavy rubber-soled boots. The footprints led past the Weaving Unit and the Printing Room to a row of sheds, most of them firmly locked. The door of the last shed was slightly ajar.

A body speared by a dagger. Blood. A masked man with a gun.

Steeling herself for the sight of something dreadful, Serena sidled in. As her eyes grew accustomed to the dark, she saw enormous cans of vegetables, catering tins of coffee, packets of tea, rice, sugar, and wide racks of cooking utensils.

"Irene?" she called.

Something clattered in the corner of the storeroom, making her jump. Quietly picking her way in the gloom, Serena found Irene, mouth covered with chocolate, clutching a packet of crisps in one hand and an apple in the other.

Throwing down the crisps, Irene burst into hysterical sobs.

"I'm so hungry," she wailed.

"It's OK," Serena said. "Come on, let's get you out of here. We'll clean you up and go for a walk by the sea."

The creak of a closing door made her run back to the entrance, but it was too late. She tugged at the handle but the door was firmly locked. The only light in the store came from a tiny window, high up in the wall.

"Oh, Lord, we'll both die here," screeched Irene. "It's all my fault. If I wasn't so greedy... We'll run out of air, we'll starve."

Raising an eyebrow, Serena gestured to the racks of food, and Irene began to laugh. Tears poured down her cheeks, smearing the chocolate. Serena took a bottle of water from the shelf and poured it over a tissue she found in her pocket.

She looked round while Irene wiped her face.

"OK," said Serena, "What we'll do is this. You get cups, candles, coffee and matches from the shelves. I'll find water and biscuits, a kettle and fuel. We'll build a little fire over there, near the door. Then we'll have a hot drink, something to eat, and wait. Artie'll come looking for me soon. And if not, someone'll be along in the morning. We've got enough air, more than enough food, we'll be fine."

She knew Artie would come for her. Despite his dumb sense of humour, he was always there, steady and loving.

There was a metal bin near the wall. Breaking up a few empty cardboard cartons, Serena shook some barbecue charcoal from a sack into the cast iron container. She soon had a fire glowing in the bin, and water heating in a kettle.

They sat by the fire with coffee and biscuits, smoke wisping round them.

"We do this a lot at home," Irene said. "Barbies."

"We used to do the same when I was a kid," Serena said. "There was always a fire going outside the trailer. Ma would make the most delicious stew. I miss those days." Serena cleared her throat. "There were twelve of us, always someone shouting or playing the mouthorgan, something always going on. Summers, we used to travel round farms in Cambridgeshire, fruit picking, helping with the harvest, but that's all finished now. We've been replaced by machines or cheap foreign labour. And moving around in a trailer's a joke. There's nowhere to stop, and the roads are so busy. That way of life is almost dead, killed off. Me and Artie tried living on a municipal caravan site for a bit, but it felt like a jail. So we settled in a house. But I miss the freedom."

To her surprise she heard herself add, "I want to start a family. But I can't imagine bringing up a child so far from my relations. Sometimes it gets so lonely!"

Irene took another biscuit and gave Serena a searching glance. "If it's the right time for a baby, it doesn't matter where you live. You'll bond with other young mothers, or move nearer to your folks. There's always a way."

Perhaps Irene's right, she thought. Maybe it is time. Perhaps the Alien Princess is a sign of the future.

She thought she could hear a child crying in the distance, and instinctively cradled her arms. The air was filled with the sweet smell of milk.

Irene fed the empty biscuit packet into the fire, and the blaze flared up. "I cry when I think about my childhood," she smiled wistfully. "But not because it was nice. I try to forget about it, to be honest. My dad was evil. He beat us if we made a noise or spilt something. He was a horrible man, always drunk, bullied my mum and my little brothers. I felt so scared and so helpless. I suppose that's why I still feel useless and ugly and clumsy, all these years later."

"You're a very attractive woman," Serena told her. "Nice eyes, lovely skin. The fact you come over to England on your own shows you're not helpless. You're a beautiful, strong lady."

"We were dirt poor," Irene continued. "Never had enough to eat. And if we did something Dad didn't like, he'd starve us for days, lock us in the outhouse without food. That's why I eat so much now."

She sighed and shook her head. The smile had gone. Her face, in repose, was almost beautiful.

"I know where Douglas keeps the spare storeroom

key. The shop was shut and I wanted some chocolate. I felt so low after stuffing up in dancing today. Comfort eating, my therapist calls it. I'm so ashamed, stealing from the community."

Serena poured more bottled water into the kettle, and they sat companionably in the dark, their faces lit by the glowing embers.

"What happened when you grew up?"

"Got out as soon as I could, mate. Went to Art College in Sydney, studied dressmaking. Wanted to be a designer. Then I met Jeff, and we married, moved to his dad's property. So now I'm a farmer's wife, four kids, all left home."

She started to cry again. "I love it here in Scotland, at the Centre. I feel at ease, like I belong. I love the rain. I love the morning meditation in the Sanctuary. I'd love to live here. I'd work in the Pottery, or in the weaving studio. I enjoyed weaving when I was at College."

Serena handed Irene a fresh cup of coffee, wondering how much longer it would be till someone found them. She shivered as the evening started to cool.

"Tell me about this place. I don't know much about it."

"There was a woman," Irene replied. "She was commanded in a vision to come here and grow vegetables. Locals said nothing would grow on the salty soil, but it did. And then, the spirits told her to set up an educational centre for spiritual renewal."

Serena dunked a biscuit in her cup. "I just came for the dancing. I didn't realise it was going to be like this, all this tuning in and stuff."

Suddenly, Irene stuck out her hand. "Serena, tell my fortune."

Serena shook her head. "I hardly ever do readings.

It's all a load of rubbish, you know."

"Please," Irene begged. "What harm will it do?"

Her hand was large and tanned, the hand of a worker. Serena turned it over and looked at the sticky palm.

Occasionally she did readings for friends, telling them what they wanted to hear. Like a therapist, but free, Artie said. Sometimes, when the special feeling came over her, she saw patterns or signs in the hand.

As she pressed Irene's fingers, the vision of a woman in stout shoes, holding a length of woven tartan, unrolled before her eyes.

"Irene, there are going to be some radical changes in your life. You're going to stay in Europe for a few months."

"Here, in Scotland?"

"Is that what you want?"

"Yes. Like I said, I want to work in the weaving studio and make beautiful patterns." She laughed. "The first thing I'll weave will be a shawl. These Scottish evenings are really freezing. Not like Queensland. What are we going to do now? We're both shivering already, and it'll get even colder during the night."

Serena jumped up. "Come on! Let's practise that dance Paula taught us today."

Irene rose reluctantly. "I'll get it wrong."

"So what! Doesn't matter."

Serena started to hum the tune they'd danced to that afternoon. Slowly demonstrating the steps, she pulled Irene behind her. Irene stumbled, missed a beat, cursed, and joined in again. After some time, Serena sensed Irene melting into the music, becoming part of the dance. The two women wove round the candles and the fire in the semidarkness.

"This feels so good," Irene shouted. "I'm really dancing!"

Serena sighed. "The only time I feel really free is when I dance."

Voices were calling outside the door. A key turned in the lock, and two shadowy figures stood at the threshold, peering into the storeroom. The sky was deep blue behind them, studded with stars.

"Are you alright," Artie gasped, hugging Serena tightly. "I thought the Aliens had got you. I was so worried."

Douglas looked at the fire "What *have* you two been doing? Lucky Artie raised the alarm, otherwise you'd have been here all night."

"We've been dancing," Serena told him.

As she spoke, she felt an invisible finger stroke her palm, the light touch of a baby.

With a smile she added, "Dancing with angels."

The Fires of Firle

The tension had been mounting all day. Smoke from invisible fires wafted over the town, clouding the eyes. Now, as darkness fell, spectators gathered behind street barriers, holding lanterns.

From afar came the sound of brass bands, the stamp of marching feet. When the first trumpeters reached the main road, the onlookers clapped and cheered. Behind the band walked townsfolk in medieval costumes, carrying flares.

The crowd sighed.

The procession tramped past, the blazing flares throwing menacing shadows over the onlookers. Fireworks exploded, tearing the sky.

Arun shivered in the cold night air.

The *thud thud thud* of heavy boots resounded in his chest. He tried to wipe the sweat off his brow, but the pain in his arm was too sharp. He let the cold perspiration trickle down his neck.

Jenny squeezed his hand as the tableaux were paraded through the village. When a gigantic devil with a leering face and long horns went by, Keith booed and Abi squealed in her childish voice, "Look at that, Grandpa!" The hideous devil turned to the children and bowed, its jaw opening and closing, dripping blood.

"No!" screamed Arun, but his voice was lost in the jeers.

Jenny laughed at a float bearing the straw model of an unpopular politician. Arun's uneasiness heightened. The dark street, the marchers, the shouts and jeers stirred awful shadows from the past.

A louder roar went up. He stood straighter, looking over the heads of the spectators. A cardboard caravan was being carried by, with painted pictures of children's faces peering from the window. Some onlookers shouted approval, others gasped, "Shame!" Then the crowd set off behind the procession, following the effigies down to the enormous bonfire.

Arun clutched his chest and swayed. The last thing he heard that night was Jenny asking, "Arun, are you alright?"

Sixty-five years ago, there had been another caravan. Sixty-five years ago there had been other processions.

The elderly man having a heart attack in the street of Firle in East Sussex was the only survivor of a family of German Sinti Gypsies.

By the time he was liberated in 1945, five year old Arun was an arsonist.

"It's only to be expected," the psychiatrist had told the matron of the Warsaw orphanage while Arun fidgeted before them in a chair. "Fire is all he knows. He grew up with smoke belching from crematoria chimneys. His entire family was burnt to ash. By starting fires himself he takes some control over his life."

Matron nodded patiently. "I know. But I can't allow the child to go round burning documents and clothes. He's a liability. Of course I want to help him, but the other children will go up in flames at this rate!"

"I'll see what I can do. I've a friend in England. I'll write to him — perhaps a change of environment is what the lad needs."

Arun's dreams were lapped in flames. Burning, devouring nightmares swallowing parents, families, cities, worlds. Like the other children in the orphanage, he woke from screaming sleep with smoke in his eyes.

Even when he was sent to his new home in Coventry, he met English children who dreamt of fire. Of bombs, and planes engulfed in tongues of red and gold.

It was his foster father, Jim, who showed him that fire had another meaning. That fire could be a metaphor for life. That fire ritually cleansed and symbolically enlightened. Jim's full name was Professor James Hamilton of the Department of Anthropology, University of Coventry.

Instead of reading bedtime stories to his foster-son, Jim acted out excerpts from *The Golden Bough.* Arun listened intently as Jim told him about the fire-festivals of Europe and the effigies placed in flames.

"It's believed that in ancient times, real people were sacrificed," Jim told Arun one night. "To purify the community, to take away collective guilt."

"Were my family sacrificed?"

Jim planted a kiss on his foster-son's head. As the door closed behind him, Arun saw flames leaping up the wall.

He screamed so loudly, Hannah, his new mother, took him into the marital bedroom. "What on earth have you been saying to him?" she scolded Jim as Arun clung to her neck.

"Only a bit about human immolation," Jim explained sleepily. "It's cathartic, it'll get the sorrow out of him. It's just what he needs. I want him to learn that fire is connected with life and fertility, not only with death."

"Well, you're sleeping in the armchair tonight! Maybe that'll teach you to keep your ideas to yourself. The boy's suffered enough."

Tucking the sheets round Arun's thin body, Hannah lay down beside him, stroking his black hair. Comforted by the cool hand smoothing his forehead, Arun finally fell asleep.

Although bedtime stories were now restricted to adventures from *Just William* and *Biggles*, Jim still found opportunities to talk to Arun about fire. One Sunday after church, while the two of them were waiting for Hannah to dish up lunch, Jim gave Arun an impromptu test.

"Needfire!" he said, as Hannah brought a tureen of oxtail soup to the table.

"A fire to drive out illness and epidemics!" Arun smiled, spooning up a mouthful of broth. "Ask me some more."

"Solsticial fires?" Jim enquired.

"Fires built at the Midsummer or Midwinter solstice, to celebrate or revive the sun."

"Well done, son," Jim said. They both laughed.

Hannah collected the soup-plates, banging them together irritably. "Leave Arun alone, Jim!" she snapped. "Why can't you let him eat in peace? Why can't you talk about football like a normal father?"

But as she clattered the Yorkshire pudding from the oven and slid the small ration of pork onto the serving dish, Jim continued his questions.

"Solar fires?"

"Same as suncharms or solsticial fires, to ensure the sun will continue to shine."

"Good chap. Well done!"

To Arun's delight, these oral exams became a

feature of Sunday lunch. When he talked about fire, his black eyes glowed with pleasure. There was something about a blaze that drew him, warmed him. Jim once read him something about France, where in olden times, people called out to the flames. "Oh fire," they shouted, "you are my mother, Oh fire, you are my father."

Arun could understand that, he felt close to his dead parents when he crouched near the flames of the living room hearth.

When he was almost nine, he was sent to prep school, followed by Eton and Oxford. He did well — years in a half-ruined Polish orphanage made English boarding schools seem benign. Leaving people he loved was what he knew, being sent away was normal.

Eventually he got a job in a bank, and married Jenny from Accounts. They bought a house in Surbiton, and had a son. His foster-mother died in her eighties, then Jim passed away a year later. And now Arun was a grandfather, still working part-time in the bank on Outreach Programmes.

He had extinguished the past. Apart from his wife, their historian son Dave and daughter-in-law Steffi, no one knew Arun's origins. On the rare occasions when someone probed into his background, he said his ancestors were from Spain. There was no point in telling the truth. People couldn't handle it. He couldn't bear their shock.

It was Dave who'd suggested a family holiday in the South Downs. "There's an old village, Dad, mentioned in the Domesday Book. The name Firle means oak woodland in Anglo-Saxon. It's a lovely place with an interesting history. Virginia Woolf wrote about it in *To the Lighthouse*. And Abi and Keith would love you and Mum to come."

"We'll end up babysitting!" Arun warned his wife. "I'd rather stay at home."

"Well, I'm going," Jenny declared. "You stay home if you want, but I don't see nearly enough of the grandchildren! And it'll give Steffi a break, she and Dave need some quality time together."

In the end, Arun agreed, and they drove down for the week's holiday. The bed and breakfast was comfortable, and the grandchildren made him laugh. He was glad he'd changed his mind. Childhood is so short and so precious, he thought.

In the lobby of the hotel, there was a bright poster pinned to the noticeboard.

DON'T MISS THE BONFIRES OF FIRLE. PROCESSION STARTS 7.00PM

Arun remembered Jim and the fire-festivals of Europe, and the taste of oxtail soup came into his mouth.

Seeing the caravan pass by with painted faces staring from the window revived dreadful memories. Of being dragged with his brothers from the encampment. Of lorries roaring away. Of a guard hiding him in an empty bucket, smuggling him out of the concentration camp. Of the long journey to the orphanage. Of loneliness and grief and desolation. Of smoke and death.

"And how's the patient today?" asked the nurse. "You've got more colour in your cheeks this morning."

"I'm feeling better," Arun replied. "I don't know what happened, but when I saw that caravan last night, I got a pain in my arm and my chest started to burn."

The nurse checked dials and machines, noted his blood pressure. "You had a mild heart attack. You need to take it easy." On the point of leaving the cubicle, she hesitated. "I was shocked too. They went too far. I've lived in this village all my life but my father was a Romani Gypsy. Last summer some Gypsies camped nearby on a private field, there was a lot of hostility in the village. People said some of the Travellers offered to resurface their drives, but didn't do a proper job, overcharged and the like. Last night was the village's revenge — there's a tradition here of burning effigies of unpopular people. But that was going too far, it was wrong."

Picking up her pen, the nurse smiled apologetically. "Sorry, dear, I shouldn't be putting all this on you. It's not your problem."

"It's OK," Arun said. "We've all got our secrets." He leaned back on the pillow and looked at the nurse. "I'm going to report the incident to the police. Take it up with the authorities."

The nurse looked at him saying "I think you'll find someone's done that already!" Straightening up, she left the ward, swinging away with long strides.

Arun closed his eyes, waiting for visiting time, sensing ghosts of long dead relatives waiting with him, sitting on the bed.

In the afternoon, his family came with flowers and fruit.

"We're in the paper, Grandpa!" yelled Abi, bouncing on the chair.

Jenny bent over and stroked his cheek. "And on the news!" she added. "The caravan burning made the national papers. Traveller organisations are protesting and the police are involved."

"The Gypsy Council's up in arms," nodded Steffi.

"And the Commission for Racial Equality!" said Dave. "MPs are taking it up. It seems someone from the village complained. Now everyone's talking about it."

The weight in Arun's chest lightened.

The mist cleared from his eyes.

The smoke drifted away.

Lilijiana's List

1 pair socks
1 pair knickers
1 petticoat
1 undervest
1 pair trousers
1 blouse
1 jumper
1 skirt
1 exercise book
1 pen
2 pencils
comb
mirror

Lilijana stared at her list. These were the only things she was allowed to take.

Mama picked up the heavy shears. Lilijana watched her cut a faded red curtain into strips, bundle up some clothes and wrap them in one of the pieces of cloth.

Yesterday, Marko had lopped branches from the old plum tree in the garden with Papa's axe. The wood was piled in the corner of the room, underneath the icon. Mama slipped the bundle of loosely wrapped clothes over a branch, knotting the ends of curtain cloth tighter. The bundle swayed on its wooden neck, like a bloody head.

Lilijana wasn't sure if this was a dream or a nightmare.

The kettle sighed steam into the air. Mama made tea, dolloping spoonfuls of plum jam into each glass. The four of them sat silently with their memories.

The sweet taste sniped at Lilijana's mouth, and she swallowed hard. Something trickled down her cheek and plopped into her glass. Tamara gave a high harsh giggle which turned into a sob. Mama had tears in her eyes. Marko coughed.

Lilijana knew what they were thinking, what they were remembering. Every year the village children helped pick plums, going from house to house, working garden by garden, stacking ripe fruit into baskets. At every home they were given food, fresh lemon squash, biscuits warm from the oven, then, hands purpled with plum juice, they moved on to the next house, laughing, shouting.

Every summer, there was a village plum festival. The men set up tables in the clearing between the forest and the foot of the mountain, where the waterfall trickles down the crag. Villagers dressed in their best clothes, the women in white blouses with intricate designs, and red or blue skirts with heavy felt aprons patterned with vivid flowers.

Lilijana and her family were the only Romanies in the village. On feast days Lilijana put on a red satin blouse, an emerald skirt with a scarlet flounce, the outfit topped by a leaf green shawl sewn by Aunt Marina. Mama braided gold coins into Lilijana's plaits, and fastened a heavy necklace round her throat. Papa and Marko wore black silver-braided velvet waistcoats and felt hats, tucking their trousers into soft high boots.

They always walked with Szara's family to the clearing where the feast was held. The tables were laden with bonewhite boiled eggs, onions in rich tomato sauce, golden pastries filled with cream cheese and spinach, freshly baked bread. Smoke from the barbecue twisted upwards, disappearing into the mountains where the Gypsy *mahala* was situated. The village children ran shouting and laughing, collecting firewood or carrying platters of freshly barbecued chicken to the tables.

There were sweets and cakes, the sun glistening on the delicate layers of syrup and nuts. On each table, bottles of plum wine.

Before the meal, the musicians arrived from the *mahala*. Lilijana's uncles and cousins. Uncle Josefz always gave Lilijana a huge hug before greeting the villagers and sitting down with them to eat. The best moment was when the musicians unpacked their instruments and began to play. Villagers sang and danced, skirts swinging, boots stamping.

Aunt Marina was dead now. She'd been shot on her way down the mountain carrying a lump of goat's cheese and a jar of onion soup for Papa when he was ill. All the local Roma drank onion soup when they were ill, a thick broth flavoured with wild sorrel and honey, topped with sour cream.

Lilijana wanted to take her costume with her, but Mama said it was too heavy. Last week they'd wrapped their bright clothes in oilcloth, and buried them in the garden. Another funeral. They lit candles for Papa, Aunt Marina, and all the others who had died.

And now it was time to go. Mama put her glass down and looked at the children. "When we come back," she said, "when the war's over, when everything is normal again, we'll dig up our clothes and wash them.We'll have a big party, and all the villagers will turn out for the feast and everything will be as it was. We'll invite the whole *mahala*. We'll sing and dance..."

Lilijana knew they'd never come back, that nothing would ever be the same. And even if they did return, their clothes wouldn't fit.

She thought sadly of her flower-patterned shawl and blouse. Of the velvet waistcoats. Of Mama's lovely dress. The mountain spirits will dance in our costumes beneath the golden moonlight, she told herself.

She took another sip of tea.

1 pair socks
1 pair knickers
1 vest
1 pair trousers
1 blouse
1 jumper
1 skirt
1 exercise book
1 pen
2 pencils
comb
mirror

This was her list. This is what she was taking with her.

This time last year, before the village feast, they'd all sat in the kitchen drinking fruit juice. Papa had held his glass up to the light, admiring the deep red liquid. "Blood of the plum. So sweet it leaves a bitter aftertaste in your mouth. You can never drink enough of it to slake your thirst."

She loved listening to Papa talk. Like a poet, with lots of long words he'd taken from stories and songs.

It was time to go, to leave Szara, her best friend. They were almost the same age, and strangers always thought they were sisters, with their large dark eyes and long black hair. Lilijana loved plaiting Szara's fine hair, weaving it round and round and catching it up with a clip, threading a plum leaf into the plait. Her own hair was so heavy it wouldn't stay up, so Szara brushed it straight back, fastening it with a vine tendril.

"We're such good neighbours, like a mirror and its reflection," Mama often said. The two families celebrated and mourned together, as if there were no garden wall between them, no dividing line. The fathers worked on farms, mending machinery or tending animals, the mothers rolled out fine layers of baklava pastry on a huge board on the terrace, taking turns to add a new layer to the cake.

Even their languages merged into one, making a new tongue. Sometimes Lilijana didn't know what language she was talking, Romanes or Serbian. They shared feasts and festivals.

She felt as if her heart was going to break.

She stared out of the window. She couldn't leave. She'd spent her life with Szara, sharing secrets, doing homework under the olive tree, lying on sun-warmed earth, watching crickets dance in patches of light. Together they'd collected branches to make *duduks*, boring through the wood and drilling sound holes with Papa's awl. Lilijana had carved decorations down the side of the pipes, flowers with long curling leaves, a design her grandfather had shown her when she stayed in the mountains one summer.

They stained the pipes a matt purply colour by

boiling plums in an old saucepan, and painting the strained liquid onto the wood. The *duduks* smelt of stewed fruit, sweet and sugary. To fix the colour they'd simmered almonds from the north field in milk. The cooled liquid produced a hard, shiny glaze which smelt of nuts. Szara had learned this from her father — it's how the men varnished wood in their area. They said it was a method brought in by the Ottoman Turks.

Every night they practised their *duduks*, teaching each other tunes. At the last plum festival they played a duet, and everyone clapped and said how unusual it was to see girl musicians. They played two tunes, one that Papa used to sing, and one that Szara's mother had taught them.

Lilijana smiled at the memory, wondering if she'd ever see plum festival again. Then she read through the list for the last time.

    1 pair socks
    1 pair knickers
    1 petticoat
    1 undervest
    1 pair trousers
    1 blouse
    1 jumper
    1 skirt
    1 exercise book
    1 pen
    2 pencils
    comb
    mirror

She wrapped the clothes she was taking in a strip of curtain. She slipped her bundle over one of the branches from the plum tree.

"Don't go!" Szara had begged. "Let's run to the mountains, stay with your family there. Later, when we're old enough, we'll live where we want."

But the sound of gunfire had come closer and closer, and now the *mahala* was empty. It was too dangerous for Roma families to stay in the area. Especially after Papa had been killed.

"If the soldiers come to our village," Mama said, "they'll be looking for Gypsies. They'll rape and murder anyone who tries to help us."

Lilijana had heard the stories of slaughters and burnings. She knew they had to go, but how would her feet take her from her village? How could she leave everything and everyone she loved and understood?

"I can't believe what's happening!" she burst out, banging her empty glass on the table. "Why's everything changed? Last year we were all so happy. We went to school and ran into each other's houses without a thought. And now everyone looks embarrassed and all the doors are closed."

Mama wiped her eyes and shrugged.

Szara's father said it was a blight. "Some years," he'd told her, "for no reason, the plum trees seem to sicken and the plums don't ripen. Then you have to prune the trees so they'll thrive again the following year."

Lilijana had seen Papa pruning trees. He sharpened his axe before making a clean slice between trunk and branch. The tree wept sap-white tears and the chopped branch made a sound like a sigh. The leaves quivered and rustled and drooped. The tree went on living but the scar was always there — months later there was still a light weal on the bark.

There was a gentle knock at the door and Szara's family crowded in, smelling of cooking and wood fire, and of tears. They were carrying packages of food. "Something for the journey," said Szara's mother.

Weeping, they all embraced each other. When Lilijana held Szara, she felt something ooze from her heart.

"I'll never find another friend like you," she sobbed.

"I'll play my *duduk* every night at sunset," Szara said softly, "and you must do the same. So we'll always be together, playing the same tunes, remembering."

Mama took little Tamara by the hand. Marko picked up two bundles, Lilijana carried the food and her clothes. She didn't feel anything now, neither sadness nor fear. She calmly followed Mama into the yard, into the hazy sunset, through the deserted dusty streets. There were bodies lying in the ochre dust, bodies with purple stains. The plum branch dug into her shoulder, the bundle bumped her back.

Left, right, left, right. As she walked, a song came into her head.

We walk over mountains, through mud and through snow
Thousands of people, the old and the slow.
And the children ask, "Mama, why must we go?"
"My plum blossom," weeps Mama. "I don't know!"

1 pair socks
1 pair knickers
1 petticoat
1 undervest
1 pair trousers
1 blouse

1 jumper
1 long skirt
1 exercise book
1 pen
2 pencils
comb
mirror

That was her list. That is what she was taking with her. Plus the pipe her best and dearest friend, her Szara, who she would never see again, gave her for Eid or Easter or Djurdjevdan — she couldn't remember when. The pipe carved with Gypsy leaves and blossom, stained with the juice of the plum, and varnished with almonds stewed in milk.

The pipe she would play each sunset, wherever she was, remembering the sweet music of her mountains, the blood red plums on the tree.

A Mass for Danny

It's a year ago today. I can't believe life could change so quickly. One minute we're happy, despite the problems. And then, the blackness.

The problems, I call them. Just the usual things. Getting moved on. Trying to get the *chavies* into school. Trying to find fresh water after the standby tap's been turned off. Getting hold of a bit of food when the local stores won't serve us. Finding a doctor who won't turn us away. Keeping clean, washing clothes, just the usual.

When we first moved onto the site, things was difficult. But then everything calmed down a bit. Some of the locals seemed quite friendly, though a couple of them spat at us and called us names. Now I can see it was the calm before the storm. But we was quite happy. Jobi had a job down the village, asphalting the drive of a local bigwig from one of them big, *kushti* houses. And then the *rai* asked him to clear the trees behind the mansion, so we always had wood for the fire. Not bad *vongar*, and Jobi's not much of a drinker, used to bring most of the money back to me.

We'd had a good feed that night, the night it happened I mean. A year ago to the day, like I said. It was a fine evening, the kettle was fair singing away over the *yog*. I'd cooked a sweet pudding, the children's favourite, for afters. Then Jobi made the tea, thick and strong. I watched him punch holes in the condensed milk can, his arms like copper in the moonlight. Then he starts to sing, one of the old tunes, and slowly, one by one, the whole *atchin tan* joins in, till it's like a choir scattered round the field. Magic. A lovely memory.

And that's when the clock stopped. When the moon began to weep. When the stars shuddered in the black sky. When my heart broke.

Well, it wasn't exactly then. The *chavies* got into bed, and I changed Carmela and popped her in the cot. It was a humid evening, fair sweaty it was, so after we said goodnight to the kids, me and Jobi sat outside for a bit.

If I'd have known what was going to happen, I'd have kept Danny by me, hugged him to my chest, even if he was nearly eleven and a man. But I never knew what was coming next. Never imagined for a moment that it could happen in England, not now, not in these days.

They say us Gypsies has the second sight. Well, I never felt nothin' at all. Just contented like, at peace with the world. With my lovely man, me fine kiddies, a full stomach and the sweet taste of sticky condensed milk in me mouth.

After a while, it starts getting cold. We slips into the trailer, past the little ones, checking to make sure Carmela's OK, and then into the back, into bed. We cross ourselves, like we always do, and ask for a blessing on our home and family.

Sweet Mother Mary, forgive me for asking, but what good did that do? May Jesus and all His saints preserve me, but I can't help thinking these things. Jobi says it's the tablets making me *dinili*. Maybe he's right. Father Michael, he's the priest what comes to visit, he says it's the will of God. He says God loved our Daniel so much he took him to Heaven.

When I think back to that night, it's like a story I've heard many times before. A nightmare from the start of time. A tale that's been told for hundreds of years. And this is how it happened.

First thing I remember is dreaming of a boat in a stormy sea. Up and down, rising and falling on the raging waves. The wail of a ship's siren. Then, the sound of children screaming.

I open me eyes. The trailer's bouncing up and down. "A gale's blown up!" I shouts to Jobi. "Get the kids!"

"That's no gale," yells he, eyes glittering. "That's the *gavvers*. Them's police sirens..."

We run to the kids. The *chavies*, they're out of bed, crying and hollering. Carmella, the baby, she's standing up in her cot, laughing at her brothers and sisters. I grabs her up and wraps her in a blanket.

We've been turfed off *tans* before, but never like this. Never with so many police dogs and batons. Never with the vans being smashed to smithereens. Annie was pulling at a *mush* from the village, and he pushed her away. Old Matthew was waving his stick, trying to hit out at a bailiff. The bailiff shoved him and Matthew hit the ground.

Then suddenly, Jobi's in the thick of it. My hero. "Leave us alone!" he yells. "Why are ye persecuting us? We're only trying to live in peace. We just want a place to stay, is that too much to ask?"

And then everyone's at it, contractors, *gavvers*, bailiffs, villagers. Our men and women, biting and scratching, throwing whatever they can lay their hands on, trying to save their *chavies* and their property. Vans and trailers rolling this way and that, as if they'd come to life and were dancing some crazy dance.

Nobody saw it happen. There were no witnesses. All I know is what with all the pushing and shoving, our Danny gets run over by a *vardo*. Dead. *Mullered*. My lad. My darling lad.

We buried him in style. Gypsies and Travellers came from far and wide. Even a bloke from some University in London, he's famous, so they say, and all the high-ups from the Gypsy Council and Travellers' Organisations. Foreign Gypsies too. All come for my Danny.

We sung his favourite songs, "Can you rokker Romani?" and one he was always playing on his harmonica. "Black Eyes," a Russian Gypsy song, so they tells me.

"I'm learning this song for you, Ma," he used to say, "because of your *shukar* black *yoks*."

And sometimes when I sits near his grave, I can hear him playing.

"I can't believe it, Danny darling," I says to him, stroking his picture and the cross carved on his headstone. "I can't believe you're gone."

"I've not gone, Mammie," I hear him whisper. "I'll be here for ever and ever."

When I close me eyes, he plays that grand little tune of his, over and over.

Glossary
Romani language unless specified

atch	stop
atchin tan	stopping place
atch poggering mandi	stop bullying me
chavies	children
dicked	saw
dinili	crazy
dordie	Lord!
duduk	a pipe played in the Balkans
Far (Norwegian)	Father
gadge (plural)	non-gypsies
gadjo	non-Gypsy man
gavvers	policemen
genever (Dutch)	alcoholic drink
Gorjer	non-Gypsy man
jell	go
kamali shay	pretty girl
kolkhoz (Russian)	communal farm in Soviet times
koshti bok	good luck
mahala	Gypsy area in Balkan towns or villages
Mor (Norwegian)	Mother
mullered	killed
mush	guy
pen	sister

rai	rich man
rakli	non-Gypsy girl
rawnie	woman/lady
Reisende (Norwegian)	Traveller
rokker	speak
Romanichal	English Gypsy
shukar	lovely
tans	places
vardo	caravan/wagon
vongar	money
yog	fire
yoks	eyes